WHERE SHOULD I PUT THIS WOODPECKER?

Stories, Poems, and Shopping Lists

Aaron N. Hall

This book is for anyone
who has ever lost something
they loved

CONTENTS

FOREWORD

This book has been a weird journey.

I started assembling ideas for stories and poems, then my dad passed. He had struggled with cirrhosis of the liver for two years, and after too many diets and unsuccessful surgeries, he decided he was done with it all. Three weeks later, he was gone.

At the time, I decided to make this book about loss—sort of in honor of my dad and a way to help me process some feelings. But as I wrote poems and stories focused on loss, it felt forced. I wasn't getting what I needed from it. After all, I wasn't *healed* from my grief, so how could I write profound insights on it?

I decided to take a step back and instead wrote short stories and poems about whatever I wanted—robots, magicians, killer clown dolls, doomsday devices, yadda yadda yadda. And wouldn't you know it? I found traces of grief in nearly everything I wrote.

The pain of loss comes in a lot of different forms—a loved one passes on, failure, friends coming and going, toys getting broken, etc. It's woven into the fabric of our lives in varying calibers. Writing these stories and poems kind of reminded me of that.

So here we are. There and back again. A book about loss that stopped being about loss but never actually stopped being about loss.

Enjoy.

STORIES

DON'T TOUCH ME ELMER

Snow trickled onto Cooney-Morrissett Drive as George watched from the comfort of his living room, eyes drifting to a nearby streetlamp that illuminated the falling flakes. He wore a sweater and he nursed a cup of coffee while he slouched on the couch.

A few feet away, his son, Timmy, tore gift wrap from a box. Lillian, George's wife, sat next to him on the couch, matching his satisfied grin and resting her hand on his knee. George took a sip from his coffee and looked around the living room. The Christmas tree twinkled in the corner, and all around the floor were bits of wrapping paper and overturned toys.

Timmy was working on the last one, the big one—the crème de la crème. George watched with amusement as Timmy revealed the toy he had spent the last two months begging for. It came in a bright yellow box, and on that box was a picture of a doll with big eyes, a red nose, a goofy smile, and a clown costume.

"Wow, you got it!" Timmy exclaimed. His finger traced

the title on the box. "Don't… Touch… Me… Elmer."

George frowned. He turned to Lillian and whispered. "Don't Touch Me Elmer? I thought I got the Tickle Me Elmer."

"There are two kinds," Lillian whispered back. "The Tickle Me Elmer laughs and wiggles when you touch it. The Don't Touch Me Elmer is supposed to teach consent and personal space. You should have read the box a little closer, Georgie."

George swallowed then cleared his throat and leaned forward. "Sorry, kiddo, if that's not the one you want, we can take it back to the store tomorrow and trade it in. What do you think?"

Timmy hardly listened. He was already opening the box with tiny, eager fingers. He pulled out the doll and flipped the switch on its back, and its plastic eyes illuminated.

Timmy turned it around and studied it. "So what does it d—"

"Put me down!" Elmer commanded. Its mouth and face didn't move. It spoke through a small, tinny speaker somewhere in its body.

Timmy dropped Elmer and its little arms flopped to its sides. The child's eyes misted and his bottom lip quivered, betrayed by his new toy.

Lillian knelt on the ground beside him. "I think you need to ask it first." She consulted the instructions on the back. "Yep, it's voice activated, Timmy. Why don't you ask him if you can pick him up?"

Timmy sniffled. "Elmer, can I pick you up?"

"Yes, you may!" the doll said through its little speaker.

Hesitantly, Timmy put his hands around Elmer's middle and lifted it. He braced himself for another rebuke, but it didn't come. As a matter of fact, the doll giggled as Timmy turned it in his hands.

"Haha!" Elmer giggled. "You're my bestest best friend!"

Timmy's hurt evaporated. He laughed with Elmer and even gave the doll a hug. Lillian slid George a looks-like-Christmas-is-saved look. George watched the spectacle with confusion and relief. He leaned back and took another sip of coffee. *They're making dolls to teach kids consent and personal space now? So you have to ask it every time you want to play with it? And to think I used to play cops and robbers with sticks and rocks.*

For the rest of the morning, Timmy didn't go anywhere without Don't Touch Me Elmer. Timmy wanted Elmer to join them at the table for breakfast, and Lillian allowed it since it was Christmas. George couldn't help but glance at the doll, with its wide plastic eyes fixed unblinkingly on him. He knew the doll wasn't actually *looking* at him, but something about it still put him ill at ease.

"Don't you think it's a little odd?" George asked Lillian as they washed the dishes together.

"Of course I do." Lillian shrugged. "But I don't think it's a bad thing to teach kids consent and personal space at a young age."

"I agree, it's just… I have a weird feeling about that doll," George muttered. "Why did they have to design it like a clown? It's creepy."

"Yeah, it is," Lillian laughed quietly. "But Timmy loves it. Like, a lot. So maybe we just call this Christmas a success? Pass me the towel."

By early afternoon, Timmy had worn himself out playing with Elmer and fell asleep in the middle of the living room. George went to work tiptoeing around his son, picking up ignored toys and wrapping paper fragments. He carefully walked each toy to Timmy's bedroom to drop them into his toy chest. The last toy was Don't Touch Me Elmer, laying on its back, staring up at the ceiling with wide, lifeless eyes. As soon as George picked it up, it activated.

"Stop!" the toy complained. "Put me down! No!"

George ignored it. It was just a toy, after all. It could whine all it wanted, but in the end, it was just a sophisticated collection of wires and sensors framed inside a doll-shaped housing. The toy didn't stop yapping until George dropped it into the toy chest and slammed it shut. Then he retreated back to the living room to read a book.

He didn't look up for nearly an hour as Timmy napped. Then Timmy stirred and groaned.

"Hey, Elmer," he said blearily. "Can I pick you up?"

"Yes, you may!" Elmer's electronic voice responded.

George's eyebrows bent. *I put that thing away.* He looked up from his book, and there it was. Elmer wasn't in Timmy's toy chest. It was sitting right next to Timmy, waiting for him to wake up. What was even more unsettling was that Elmer was facing George—watching him.

Timmy scooped Elmer into a great big hug. "I love you, Elmer!"

"Haha!" Elmer responded. "You're my bestest best friend!"

Elmer's shiny little eyes never left George. A shiver slid down George's back and he went to another room to finish his book.

That night, as Lillian and George climbed into bed, George said, "I think I might be losing my mind."

Lillian smiled teasingly. "I could have told you that."

"When I was cleaning up Timmy's toys, I swore I put that Elmer doll in his toy chest. But an hour later, it was right next to Timmy, waiting for him to wake up. And I swear to goodness that it was *watching me*."

"Oh, yeah. You're definitely losing it." When George

didn't laugh, Lillian's smile drooped from teasing to concern. "George, you don't think that thing is actually alive, do you?"

George didn't respond. He just shrugged, realizing how silly it sounded.

Lillian slid deeper into the covers and sighed. "My dear husband, let's not forget that we once spent half an hour looking for your car keys before you realized you had put them in the wrong pocket. You probably just forgot to put the doll away."

But George *knew* he put that doll away. He remembered it protesting as he took it into Timmy's room. Did he just imagine it? There's no way the toy just got up on its own and made its way back to Timmy.

Right?

The day after Christmas was the same. Timmy carried Elmer everywhere, as long as he got permission first—which he always did. During Timmy's afternoon nap, George cleaned up his toys and moved them to Timmy's toy chest. The last, of course, was Elmer.

"Stop! Let go! No!"

The doll fussed through its tiny speaker as George carried it to Timmy's toy chest. He opened the lid but held Elmer up to his face to look hard into those shiny plastic eyes. For a few seconds, Elmer became quiet.

"You're not alive," George said half to the doll and half to himself. "You were made in a factory in Thailand. You're just a collection of electronics stuffed into a doll. You don't scare me."

To assert his dominance, he held Elmer tight and shook it around for a second. Then he dropped Elmer into the box and slammed it shut. When he went back to his book, he decided to enjoy it in the master bedroom with the door closed. Even as he read, he kept turning his ear toward the door to see if he could hear the cheap speaker. But it stayed quiet for over an hour. Elmer didn't make noise until George heard the muffled sounds of Timmy opening his toy chest and asking Elmer if he could pick it up.

George breathed a relieved sigh and went back to his book.

He didn't see Elmer again until 2:00AM.

George's bladder woke him up. He carefully hobbled into the master bathroom to relieve himself. After he washed his hands, he dragged his feet back to bed. But before he could even reach the mattress, he saw it.

The bedroom door had somehow opened while he was in the bathroom. And there, looming in its threshold, was the twelve-inch, clown-shaped personage of Don't Touch Me Elmer silhouetted against the hallway nightlight.

And the doll was holding a meat cleaver.

George yelped and grabbed a bedside lamp. Lillian jolted awake just as George's fumbling fingers turned the lamp on. The room flooded with dim orange light. Elmer collapsed, limp and lifeless, knife beside it.

"What, what!?" Lillian gasped. She looked all around through a curtain of frizzy hair. "George, what's the matter?"

George gave laser eyes to his wife as he jabbed a finger toward the doll laying in the threshold. Lillian had to blink hard before her eyes came into focus, but when she saw it, her face turned pale.

"I went to take a leak and when I came back to bed, that thing was *standing* in the door with that knife. As soon as I turned on the light, it went limp. Like in *Toy Story*. I think that thing wants to kill me, Lil. And it's probably because I picked it up without asking."

Lillian gave her husband a severe look. "George, if this is your idea of a prank, it's not funny."

"My darling," he replied delicately. "Love of my life… my sun and moon and stars. You know how much I enjoy teasing you, but I draw the line at psychopathic clown dolls." He pointed at it again. "I'm putting that thing back in the box and returning it. I'll pick up a Tickle Me Elmer like Timmy wanted in the first place." He found his robe and shoved his arms through the sleeves. "ShopMart opens at six. I'll be there when it opens."

From the nervous look on her face, Lillian was still assessing the situation. Either that doll was actually possessed, or her husband was a total nut job. The second explanation felt more likely, but Elmer *was* laying in her doorway with a meat cleaver.

Not knowing what else to do, she said, "Okay. Do whatever you think is best. Timmy is going to be devastated, though. He loves that doll."

"He'll get over it," George said.

George grabbed Elmer by the neck and carried it as he went out to the trash bin and fished out Elmer's box. As he went, Elmer griped with its usual phrases. But George wasn't having it. Every time it started to protest, he gave the doll a good shake, and that shut it up. He shoved Elmer back into its box, closed the lid, and taped it shut for good measure.

He got fully dressed and armed himself with the meat cleaver Elmer meant to use on him. Then he set the box down in the living room and watched it. It never moved. And all the while, George stared at it. To fill the silence, he muttered to himself.

"Stupid doll," he whispered. "Stupid doll trying to kill me. I must be going nuts. I'm losing my mind. I'll feel so much better when this thing is gone."

"You'll never be rid of me."

George's blood ran cold. It was Elmer's little speaker,

muffled by the cardboard encasing it. At first, he thought he imagined it, but Elmer kept speaking.

"I don't like being touched, George," it said. "Not without asking. Timmy is kind to me. He asks me first. But not you. You shake me and say unkind things. That hurts my feelings. Well, my feelings won't be the only thing getting hurt, George. That's a promise. And I keep my promises."

George bolted off the couch and snatched up the box. He held it between his palms and put his nose against the cardboard. His words came through gritted teeth. "In a few hours, you're going to be out my life forever! I'm ten times your size! You have no power here! Now shut up before I cut you up like you were going to cut me up!"

He jammed the box onto the ground. And for the next few hours, Elmer didn't move or make a peep. George threw the box in the trunk at 5:45AM and drove it to ShopMart.

The ShopMart parking lot was still dusted with fresh snow when he arrived. George parked near the front and was the first customer inside when the doors opened. All the while, he carried Elmer's box like it was something radioactive.

He blinked hard against the fluorescent lights and made a beeline for the customer service desk. He was greeted by a sleepy, pimply teenager who fought off a huge yawn as George approached.

"Hi, welcome to ShopMart," he said lazily. "How can I help you?"

"I need to make a return." George slammed the box on the counter. "Everything is in the box, so I should be able to at least get store credit, right?"

The teenager saw the box, and his eyes snapped open. "Oooh, you got a Don't Touch Me Elmer. Good thing you brought this back." He immediately went to work opening the box.

George stepped back. "What do you mean? Is there a problem with them?"

The teen laughed. "I'll say. Some of them have a big defect. If you don't ask before you touch them, they'll try to kill you with whatever they can get their hands on. They're pure evil. You didn't see the big recall announcement on the news?"

Dumbfounded, George replied, "I guess I missed that one."

"Crazy that no one found these in quality assurance," the teen said. "Don't worry. We'll take care of it."

The teen took Elmer out of the box, which immediately complained with its little speaker. But the teen didn't pay attention to the nos or put-me-downs. He pinned Elmer to the table with one hand, and with the other hand, revealed a large wooden mallet.

Smash!

George flinched as the employee turned Elmer's head into a crater. Bits of plastic and wires went every direction. The teen gave the decrepit Elmer a shake to make sure it didn't talk anymore. It didn't. Without looking, he hurled Elmer over his shoulder into a massive waste bin. Then he flashed a smile at George.

"That outta do it," he said. "If you want to pick up a Tickle Me Elmer, just show them your receipt at the register. Anything else I can do for you?"

George shook his head, too stunned to speak.

"Alright, mister. Have a ShopMart day."

Lillian could hardly believe it when George got home and told her the story. She made him some hot tea to calm his nerves. Timmy, however, was devastated when they told him the news. Lillian was right. When the child found out his beloved Don't Touch Me Elmer was taken back to the store, his sobs came freely.

"He's *gone?*" Timmy moaned. The tears streamed down his little face and the words came through gasps.

"I'm sorry, honey," Lillian said as she squatted down. "He was broken. But look! We got you a Tickle Me Elmer, just like you asked! This one will be much better. Okay?"

That didn't cheer Timmy up. He scowled at the box before he stomped out of the room. George and Lillian heard his bedroom door slam, followed by muffled sobs.

They deflated and exchanged sighs. George said, "You talk to him. I'll get breakfast started."

Lillian patted George on the back and went to console their grieving child. George put some bacon and eggs on the stove. And for the rest of the day, things proceeded as normal. Timmy moped and murmured. He tried to give Tickle Me Elmer a chance, but it wasn't the same as the Don't Touch Me Elmer. For some reason, the kid liked a toy that would talk to him instead of just laugh when he touched it. George didn't understand it, but what could he do? Kids like what they like.

That night, they went to bed and George hoped that Timmy would feel better in the morning. Maybe he would warm up to the Tickle Me Elmer. Thankfully, that toy wouldn't try to turn their house into a crime scene, and that made George sleep a little easier.

What he didn't know was that down the street, a figure was creeping down the sidewalk of Cooney-Morrissett Drive, limping through the shallow snow. Its image grew in the streetlight, casting a dark shadow—twelve inches tall, wearing a worn clown costume, its plastic face smashed to oblivion.

THE MERRY MEN COLLECTIVE

William found himself at his favorite bar just like he did every Friday night. Another week of riding a keyboard late into the evening while deadlines loomed and management breathed down his neck. William knew his girlfriend would be suspicious of him when he got home—work had been so stressful, bar visits after already-late hours had become frequent. She had accused him of seeing another woman, but William's only mistress was a large stack of incomplete files.

But that wasn't entirely accurate. William's *real* mistress was an obtuse, short-tempered man named Sheldon Winkler, and their relationship was parasitic. Sheldon Winkler's hairline had been receding from his piggish face since he was nineteen years old. He was physically ugly, sure, but his mind and spirit were even worse.

William had reported faithfully to Sheldon Winkler for six years and never once received a raise. Although the company boasted record profits year over year, Sheldon Winkler made sure William and his teammates never got a slice of it. It was all in the name of efficiency.

It wouldn't be as bad if Sheldon Winkler was in the trenches with the rest of his team working long hours. But instead, he would spend two or three days a week golfing or enjoying day trips. He loved showing his subordinates pictures of his most lavish vacations—Athens, Cancun, Paris—almost as if to assert dominance. Every vacation photo came with a twinkle in his eye that said, *I can do this because you work for me.* William nodded and smiled and ooh'ed and aah'ed, but in his mind he was wrapping his hands around Sheldon Winkler's pudgy little neck.

Sheldon had shown William a new batch of golfing photos today, and William had been complaining to the bartender about it. The bartender affirmed his complaints with, "That's tough," and "You got that right," and, "He sounds like a real heel." But William was perplexed when the bartender set William's drink down. There was a business card underneath the glass. William frowned and pulled it out. On ivory card stock, it had thin, solid black letters.

THE MERRY MEN COLLECTIVE: GET WHAT YOU DESERVE. On the back was a QR code.

"What is this?" William asked.

The bartender shrugged. "Beats me. Someone must have left it."

Strange. William didn't remember this card being here when he sat down. He thought about debating its existence with the bartender, but he was too tired to pursue it.

What he wasn't too tired for was curiosity. He pulled his phone out and scanned the QR code. Automatically, his phone downloaded an app (simply titled MMC) and opened it. William watched with mild panic as the phone took a mind of its own. He couldn't close out of the application, no matter how he pressed or swiped. The phone wouldn't even turn off.

What it did do was pull up a map of William's area—about a ten-block diameter. William saw a blinking dot that represented himself at the bar. And there was another blinking dot two blocks away. The map marked a trail between him and the second dot. A destination.

William drummed his fingers on the table, frowning, heart thumping with worry. Whoever left this card wanted him to *go* wherever this second dot was. He stared at it for a long while, debating. Maybe it was the alcohol stilling his inhibitions, but something inside him felt recklessly inquisitive. He took another sip of his drink, paid, and left.

Outside, the city hummed as night settled. He passed the occasional local that walked too quickly for a conversation. All the while, he kept focused on the trail the mysterious app spelled for him.

He arrived at the dot. It was a high-rise office building that had to be fifty stories tall. And it was dark on the inside. But a notification bubble popped on the screen: SCAN TO UNLOCK.

William noticed the key fob plate by the door. He held his phone to it. It flashed green, and the office door clicked. He didn't enter right away. Instead, he looked around as if to find someone spying on him, like someone was going to jump out and tell him he was on TV. But no. The street stayed quiet and dim. Hesitantly, he opened the door and slipped inside. The door closed behind him and locked again.

ASCEND TO 49th FLOOR. That was the next notification. William slowly moved toward an elevator and once again used the app to unlock a key fob. When the elevator dinged and the doors flew open, no one was inside, but it was well lit with bright fluorescent lights.

William crept in, pressed 49, and cracked his knuckles. He didn't know why he did this—maybe he thought this was an elaborate scheme for someone to rob him and he'd have to defend himself. But someone with the power to hack his phone could probably steal his money digitally without a problem. This whole thing didn't make any sense.

The elevator whirred as it ascended. When William arrived at the 49th floor, the elevator doors opened. He was in the lobby of an office suite, and the main door had large letters sandblasted onto the glass.

THE MERRY MEN COLLECTIVE—the same words from the mysterious business card. Through the sandblasted door, the office was dark, but clusters of desks and cubicles spanned the entire floor.

William crossed the lobby and peered through the glass. There looked to be a dim light on the opposite end of the floor—likely from someone's personal office. He wondered if the door in front of him was unlocked. Slowly, he reached down and turned the handle.

It was. He tried to breathe steadily as he pushed the door open. No alarms sounded. The office was utterly still. But as as soon as he stepped inside, a loud *click* echoed through the floor and a flood of fluorescent lights activated. William held his hand up to them and he blinked hard to adjust. Looking around, he took mental note that the office was frightfully bland—a bombardment of neutral colors straight out of a discount office supply store.

William frowned against it all. "The hell is this all about?" he muttered.

An intercom crackled on. William jumped. The voice on the other end said, "Good evening! Sorry, it's a bit late and my receptionist is out. If you'd like to chat, my office as at the end of the floor. Come on in."

Do I actually want to chat, though? William thought. The mysterious voice sounded friendly enough. But maybe that's why it made William even more guarded. He was on the cusp of discovering what this Merry Men Collective was, and maybe that's what made him more nervous. He had half a mind to turn on his heels and take the elevator back down. He knew he hadn't been cautious enough on his way here.

As if reading his thoughts, the intercom crackled again. "I get it. This whole thing is weird. If you want, you're welcome to leave. But you have my assurance that you have nothing to lose and everything to gain tonight. You're here because you're unhappy, and I'm sure I can make it worth your while. So if you're still interested, step into my office."

Well that *definitely* had William's attention. His feet began moving forward, independent of the conflicting thoughts that raged in his mind. At length, he reached the office within the office—clearly reserved for management.

The door was see-through glass, like the sand-blasted door by the lobby. The words on this particular door read, *Robert Holt, Founder*. William could see Robert Holt through the door, sitting at a wide mahogany desk in a big leather armchair. He was focused on a little laptop, typing furiously.

William held his breath and knocked on the door. Immediately, Robert Holt perked up and smiled. He was handsome and well-dressed, with perfectly parted hair and an expensive three-piece suit. When he stood up, William noticed he had the build of a basketball player—tall with strong shoulders and long arms.

Robert Holt crossed the room and opened the door as if welcoming William into his home.

"Come on in!" he said. "I'm Robert. Take a seat. I'm sure you have lots of questions."

Robert closed the door and snatched William's hand in a firm handshake. William stood aghast, eyes darting around the room. From the look of things, Robert definitely had a penchant for luxury. He had a mini bar equipped with several expensive liquors, multiple art pieces that appeared African in origin—but William couldn't place it—and picture frames on the wall made of gold.

"Um," William said. "What's this all about?" He held up the business card. "How did I find this under my drink?"

Robert smiled as he made his way back to his chair. "We have a way of finding those who need us most. Take a seat and we'll get started."

William didn't move. "I don't want to get started until I know exactly what this is."

Robert sat down and laced his hands together, but not before he gave William a knowing smile. "You hate your job, don't you?"

William frowned. "What?"

"*You hate your job,*" Robert repeated. "You're not getting a fair cut. Your boss is greedy. You're unhappy. And you're probably not the only one feeling it. You're a mouse running on a wheel and they're not giving you enough cheese. Sound about right?"

William's heart fell into his stomach. He gave a shallow nod. "Yeah. How do you know about all that?"

Robert gestured to a chair across from him. William finally surrendered and sat.

"Let me tell you about the Merry Men Collective," Robert said. "We're a team of highly skilled digital artisans that have a knack for getting around things. A lot of us have been burned by bosses like yours in the past, so we decided to do something about it. Assuming your employer has more than enough funds to get by, we'd like to acquire his excess and distribute it to you and your team. We will take a minor fee for our services, naturally. But you won't have to pay a dime."

William's jaw dangled. Upon realizing this, he snapped it

shut, making his teeth clack. He swallowed and said, "So, wait… you're… hackers? Or something?"

Robert Holt smiled. "Digital artisans, thank you."

"I—we—okay, even if I *did* want you to do this, this is *super* illegal."

"Legal and ethical are not the same." Robert Holt leaned back. "What is un*ethical* is withholding the proper compensation to the people who fuel your success while you stuff your mouth with money. That's not illegal, but it is *unethical.* The Merry Men Collective operates within the court of ethics. The laws of the land are less than consequential."

William raised an eyebrow. "That definitely wouldn't hold up in court."

"We've been on the receiving end of prosecution once before." Robert's eyes flashed. "The justice system won't make that mistake again."

A chill slid down William's spine. He swallowed again. "So you're telling me you can swipe money from my boss and distribute it to me and the rest of my team? And there will be no legal repercussions? What if they're able to trace this back to me?"

"They won't," Robert said as he swiveled back and forth. "We have more than enough safeguards built into our processes. All we need is a green light from you. We won't do anything without your consent—it's part of our code of conduct. But we do need a yes before we get started. So, are you in? Me and my boys would love to burn another suit. Just give me the name and the company."

A pit grew in William's stomach. All of this had happened so fast. This could go horribly, horribly wrong. He had no reason to trust this guy. He could be a masquerading lunatic for all William knew. But at the same time, the name of William's boss and employer wasn't exactly private information. Anybody could find it if they had ten minutes and a WiFi connection.

And what if Robert Holt the Merry Men Collective actually *could* do what he said they could do?

William imagined Sheldon Winkler trudging into work as a nervous wreck. He pictured it—Sheldon Winkler's tie undone, dragging his shiny loafers across the carpet, pale and distraught. No more bragging about lavish vacations or taking days off while everyone worked their fingers to the bone. He'd be just like the rest of them. William's lips twitched into a smile.

"You know what? Fine," William said. "I don't know you and I don't know if what you're saying is true, but I work for Sheldon Winkler at CJS Technologies. Do what you want." A pause. "How am I going to see the money from this?"

Robert grinned and turned to his laptop. His fingers immediately blazed across the keyboard. His mind and hands seemed to operate on different tracks. "Keep your eyes on your bank account. It won't be tomorrow, or next week, or even the week after that. But soon. That's all I need from you, friend. Good night."

William blinked and stared. That's it? *Thanks, we got it, good night?* After a few awkward seconds, Robert Holt looked up from his monitor and cocked his head toward the door, inviting William to leave. William did as instructed.

As he left the skyscraper, he wondered what things he had put in motion. He couldn't stop thinking about it during the subway ride. When he arrived home, his girlfriend was understandably upset. He tried to explain that there wasn't another woman and that he met a strange man who might bless them with serious cash, but she didn't find that explanation any more believable.

Robert was right. No money arrived the next day. Or the

next week. Or even that month. William was starting to wonder what all of that was really about. Maybe Robert Holt had played some elaborate prank on him—that thought made anger flare in William's chest. He didn't want his hardship to become someone else's amusement. William's girlfriend kept pestering him about the money, and William grew increasingly frustrated with the questioning. He felt like a fool.

Then it happened.

Robert checked his bank account on a Tuesday morning and found a deposit larger than his annual salary. He couldn't believe it. He showed his girlfriend with shaking hands, and she could barely believe it, too. They danced and screamed and kissed and hugged. Still, William had to go to work as to not raise suspicions. He got off the subway with an extra pep in his step and took the elevator to his cubicle in the CJS Technologies high-rise.

He could tell that his coworkers got it, too. Two of them were on frantic, confused phone calls when William arrived. It sounded like they were talking to their banks, asking about deposits. But no one seemed to have the answer. William smiled to himself. Looks like Robert Holt and the Merry Men Collective made good on their promise. Everyone was getting their share now. The money they received was the money they should have been receiving for years.

But Sheldon Winkler never came into work. William wanted so bad to see the look on his face, but the grubby little manager never showed up. One of his teammates asked another manager about it, and they said Sheldon had taken the day off for a personal matter. Another one of William's coworkers joked that "personal matter" was a funny way of saying "wine tasting," and everyone laughed. William knew Sheldon was probably in a panic, trying to track down his missing cash.

But one day turned to two. And two days turned to three. Sheldon didn't show all week. William's team didn't learn the fate of Sheldon Winkler until the following Monday.

Suicide.

One of Sheldon's family members found him dangling from a rafter in his penthouse apartment. A representative from upper management was sent to tell Sheldon's team.

The news made William's blood cold. The entire mood at the office took a dive. Everyone worked their typical late-hour shifts with hardly any chatter among them. Sure, no one liked Sheldon, but no one wanted to see him *dead*.

A large pang of guilt nestled in William's chest for days. He kept asking himself if this was his fault. Would Sheldon Winkler still be alive if he never followed his curiosity to the Merry Men Collective?

And that wasn't the end of his troubles. At the end of the week, another manager called an emergency meeting with his department to tell them all of their positions had been terminated. The company had recently hired a consultant from a nearby agency that recommended some downsizing, and William's department was selected. Everyone would get a pitiful severance package covering two-weeks pay. They were told to clean their desks and leave within thirty minutes.

William was a ghost for the rest of the day. He didn't take his desk knickknacks; he just left his laptop and walked out. Everything was a blur. He and his girlfriend had used that massive deposit to pay off credit cards and student debt, so there was barely a shred of it left. Now he was unemployed with no savings! They still had an apartment to pay for! In this economy, it could take months before he found another position!

He realized that he had been standing on the sidewalk,

caught up in his thoughts. He snapped himself awake and checked his phone. The Merry Men Collective app was gone. Naturally.

But he still remembered his way to the building. It wasn't far. He could confront Robert Holt himself.

He found the high rise and took the elevator up. It was still the middle of the work day, so nothing was locked. When he arrived on the 49th floor, his eyes grew wide and his heart fell into his stomach.

There was no Merry Men Collective. The door had been replaced. There were no cubicles or desks or computers inside. It was all an empty expanse. On the glass door, a FOR LEASE sign was taped with a phone number.

William stared at it, mouth agape. It had only been a few weeks. It seemed like the Merry Men Collective had been wiped from existence.

He jumped with a start as his phone buzzed in his pocket. He pulled it out to see the call was coming from an unknown number. Usually William ignored these, but he had a feeling about this one. He answered the phone and held it to his ear. "Hello?"

"You wanted to see me?"

It was Robert Holt's voice. He didn't sound high-energy and inviting like last time. He was all business now.

"Yeah," William said strongly. "What happened to your office?"

"We left. Is that all, William? I'm very busy."

William paused. "I just lost my job."

"I'm sorry to hear that."

William expected more. But upon Robert's silence, he raised his voice. "Well, what are *you* going to do about it?"

Robert tsked. "You expect me to do *anything* about it? This is outside of our agreement, William. I did exactly what

I said I would do. I took Sheldon Winkler's wealth and distributed it to you and your team. He got what he deserved, and so did you. If anything, you should be thanking me."

William started pacing the lobby floor. "Yeah, well, because of you, Sheldon Winkler is dead. He committed suicide after he lost all that money."

Robert Holt laughed. He actually *laughed*. That made William's blood pressure increase.

"What's so funny?" William demanded.

"Your boss was such a coward that he would rather be dead than poor," Robert said. "That's funny to me."

William's face was beet-red as he spoke through his teeth. "A man is dead because of what you do, Robert. Do you hear me? *Dead*. You've got blood on your hands."

"No, I don't." Robert chuckled condescendingly. "Even if I did, that would make you my accomplice, wouldn't it? You gave me his name, after all. This wouldn't have been possible without your approval. This is what's really happening: *you* feel responsible for Winkler's death, so you're trying to shift the blame to me to feel better about yourself. Don't be such a child."

That caught William's tongue. So Robert kept talking.

"Let me assuage your conscience," he said. "Neither you or I are responsible for Sheldon Winkler's death. It was a *suicide*. I didn't kill him. Neither did you. He saw his money disappear so he made the choice to off himself. He could have listened to all those inspirational grindset videos he loved so much and built himself back up, but he chickened out. Now he's gone. Sheldon Winkler died as he lived—a fragile, pathetic man. End of story."

William didn't say anything. Robert Holt's long sigh echoed through the phone.

"Don't mourn cowards and bullies, William," he said.

"Your job situation is unfortunate. But I see situations like this all the time. You're not a person to them. You're a cog, a spring, a button to be pressed. You're an interchangeable part that's scrapped when you become obsolete. Winkler helped run the machine, now he's dead. And you feel sorry for him? Don't."

"He was still a person though," William mumbled. "Being a bad boss doesn't mean you deserve to die."

"Winkler thought differently." Robert paused. "Move on, William. You got what you deserved, and the person who robbed you is gone. It's over."

William swallowed and cleared his throat. Timidly, he said, "Is there… any way you can use your computer stuff to find me a new job?"

"No."

William swallowed in a dry throat. "You know, in some ways, I think you're worse than he was."

"You're right," Robert Holt said. "I'm not a good man. I'm a smart man. I know I lectured you weeks ago about ethical versus legal, but when it comes down to it, I made a system that lets me rip off idiots for my own financial gain. So, in a way, I do exactly what they do. I just look a hell of a lot better doing it." He paused. "Are you done?"

William nodded. "Yeah."

"Good."

Robert Holt hung up. Silence filled the 49th floor lobby. As William's arms drooped to his sides, he let himself swim in his thoughts.

He didn't want Sheldon Winkler to die. He was just tired of being treated unfairly. Someone presented an opportunity to level the playing field, so William took it. Was that so wrong?

But by doing so, Sheldon Winkler was dead—a casualty

of another predator out to make a buck. And now the deposit transferred to William's account felt filthy.

William hated that he felt this way. He just wanted to get what he deserved! He didn't deserve *this*—the screaming guilt, the fear, the uncertainty.

He wished there was a lesson to be learned here, but he couldn't find it.

When he reached the bottom floor, he walked straight to his favorite bar, where this all began. He would have a lot of drinks before he went home to his girlfriend.

THE BEACON AND THE WOLF PART 1

You try to stop an intergalactic dictator from seizing power, and you end up crash landing on an alien planet. So it goes.

I need to contact the other freedom fighters. But first, I need to get out of this cryotube. It hisses open and I stagger onto the floor. Thawed cryofluid drips off me like syrup, so I clean myself with a nearby towel and throw on a fresh jumpsuit. That's when I get a look at things.

It's a good thing I was in the cryotube. Everything is in disarray and half of the ship is broken—loose wires and fractured metal are everywhere. The ship's control panel is completely crunched from impact. It's a miracle my cryotube wasn't damaged.

There's a 72-hour kit with standard emergency supplies nearby: three days of rations, a water canteen, a medpack, a tent, a space blanket, some rope, a knife, a pocket computer, a standard issue United Galaxies Armada blaster, and an emergency beacon.

Emergency beacon. Bingo. I sling the pack over my

shoulder and approach the exit hatch.

By the hatch is a universal atmospheric conversion mask so I can breathe whatever air this planet has. I shove it onto my face before I force the escape hatch open.

The hatch clatters to the ground. I step out and my eyes go wide. This place is gorgeous. The trees surrounding me stretch hundreds of meters high, ending in a flat, green canopy. Wildlife sounds all around me—a cacophony of chirping, buzzing, and hooting.

There's no time to gawk, though. I pull out my kit's emergency beacon, set it on the ground, punch a few buttons, then watch it rev up. But right as it's about to broadcast, it stops whirring and lets out three beeps.

"Poor conditions," it says. "Please select alternative location."

I frown. Alternative location? Odd. This thing can shoot a distress signal across a galaxy but it can't get its signal through a bunch of trees? These trees must be signal scramblers somehow. I sigh angrily and fold the beacon up. I just need to find a clearing or a hilltop.

I pull out the pocket computer from the emergency kit. It struggles to boot up but I finally see the main home screen. Weird—the date shows five Earth years from the time I jumped into cryosleep. I should have only been in cryo for an hour at most—that's the only way I wouldn't get hurt using hyperspeed in my tiny escape pod.

I roll my eyes. The freedom fighters are always picking up cheap secondhand gizmos. This thing probably had a wrong date when they bought it.

The pocket computer says the atmosphere is safe to breathe. I'm a little hesitant to try it out, given the date malfunction. But I chance it. I pull the breathing mask from my face just a little bit to taste this planet's air. Seems fine.

Better than fine, actually. The air is clean and cool, unlike a lot of the recycled oxygen you get on starships. I take the mask completely off, breathing deep. Still feels good. I stuff the mask into my emergency pack, then turn my attention to the pocket computer.

I select the Terrain Mapping feature, hold it up, and do my best to cover my ears. The pocket computer lets out a loud beep, then I turn forty-five degrees. Beep. Turn. Beep. Turn. I do that until I've done a full three-sixty. With the computer's sonar capabilities, it maps out all the terrain within a five-mile radius. As luck would have it, there's a small mountain about five miles away. The trees get much thinner around the base of that mountain, so it's got to be clear on top.

Halle-freaking-lujah. I unwrap a food ration and get moving.

I'm traveling at a slower pace than I would like. If it were a straight shot to the mountain, I could make that trip in a couple of hours. But even short-term cryosleep makes you feel like a zombie, and the forest floor is heavy with tall grass and fallen branches, so I'm moving much slower than I would like. After what feels like several hours of walking, I pull out the pocket computer.

"Computer," I ask it. "How far have I traveled from the crash location?"

The computer responds with a pleasant, androgynous voice. "You have traveled 2.284 miles."

Not even halfway there. I groan loudly then take a long swig from my canteen. I grimace—it doesn't taste great, but at least it's clean. It's hard to tell through the trees, but I think it's starting to get dark. And after walking for hours post-cryosleep, I think this is a good time to make camp.

The grass is too tall, so a fire is out of the question.

Thankfully the climate on this planet is pretty temperate, so it shouldn't get too cold during the night. I throw down my 72-hour kit.

A growl rumbles from behind me—a low, guttural roll.

My heart travels to my throat and the hairs on my neck prickle. I look over my shoulder with terrified slowness to see something that looks like a cross between a bear and a rhino. It has four ink-black, grapefruit-sized eyeballs fixed on me, four thick legs complete with claws, a mighty jaw with rows of sharp teeth, and rubbery blue skin.

My heart is in my throat. I swallow and click a button on my pocket computer. "Computer, what is that thing?"

The computer analyzes it with its camera. "The image is unclear, but it could be a srusorec. They can weigh approximately nearly four hundred kilograms and are considered highly territorial."

The srusorec huffs and paws at the dirt as if ready to charge. I delicately reach for my blaster.

"Can I kill it?" I ask.

"Unlikely," the computer responds. "They can charge at speeds of nearly fifty kilometers per hour. Your best chance is a well-aimed blaster shot to the head or neck. Statistically speaking, you are more likely to be mauled to death."

"Figures."

The beast roars and charges. I whip around like a gunslinger and fire two red blaster shots at its face. Misses. No time for a third. I dive out of the way just as the beast pounces. But I'm not fast enough. It catches my thigh with its long claws and tears through the flesh. I scream—it's like three hot knives ripping through my thigh. The claws missed the femoral artery, so I'm lucky in a way, but I'm still minutes away from being torn apart by Space Yogi.

I squirm on the ground and fire two more shots. First

one misses. Second one hits the srusorec in the shoulder. It roars, more pissed than hurt. Then it turns to pounce on me one last time. I'm a goner.

One more Hail Mary shot. It hits just below the jawline. The beast staggers as it begins to ooze blue blood from the smoking hole in its neck. It stumbles a bit, rocking from side to side, then, as if trying to take me down with its final movement, it tumbles toward me. I roll out of the way just before all four hundred kilograms of space bear crash onto the dirt.

I take huge breaths, trying to still my thumping heart. I spit out dirt and grass. Then I take a look at my leg. Ouch. Slick blood is all over me, and I can see flaps of torn muscle through the shreds in my jumpsuit.

I breathe shakily, trying to stay calm and remember my survival training. The first step is a tourniquet. With trembling fingers and my heart beating like a war drum, I tear a long strip of fabric from my ruined jumpsuit and tighten it around the root of my thigh with a thick stick until I can barely stand it. That stops the bleeding considerably.

Step two is to treat the laceration. I scoot toward my survival pack, using only my hands, butt, and good leg. I find the medpack and crack it open. There are a few single-use syringes inside. I grab the one for deep lacerations and an antiseptic wipe. The wipe feels like a joke against my shimmering, bloody leg, but hey, I still need to disinfect it.

With a shaky hand, I inject the fluid into little spots around the edges of my cuts. It helps deaden the pain and I know it'll accelerate the tissue growth. By morning, the leg might be completely stitched up. It's going to *hurt*, though. Tomorrow's mountain climb was already going to be bad enough, but now my leg is going to complain the whole way.

At this point, I collapse, lay on the ground for a while,

still clutching my tourniquet. I try to think of something that relaxes me. Apple pie. A warm bath. Breathe in. Breathe out.

Okay. I'm alright. I dive back into my emergency pack for my tent. It's the size of a paperback novel, with a little red button on the edge. I press the button and toss it a couple meters away. It beeps for five seconds, then puffs loudly and rapidly expands into the size of a cramped two-person tent.

Home sweet home.

"Hey, computer," I say, "any likelihood that another one of those space bears is close by?"

"The likelihood of seeing another srusorec in the next twenty-four hours is 4.23 percent," it says. "Srusorecs are highly territorial. Each one usually covers an area of 90.49 square kilometers."

"Right, you said that," I say as I give my tourniquet another tug. I wince at the pain. "Well, tell your little database that I totally kicked one's ass."

"I shall make a note of it. Thank you for your contribution."

I drag myself, and my emergency pack, into the tent, zip the entrance closed, then put my pack under my torn leg to elevate. After a few swigs from my canteen, I feel myself starting to drift, so I make another knot to keep my tourniquet in place. Then I'm out.

I awaken to diffused sunlight shining through the tent's fabric. It grazes my face until I blink hard and sit up. My mouth feels like cotton and my stomach rumbles, so I grab my canteen and a ration bar. As I start to chow down, my eyes adjust. That's when I see my thigh.

Sure, my wounds are mostly stitched up. I'll definitely have long scars from the lacerations, but on the dried blood, there are dozens of yellow bugs that have made their home on my wound seams. I groan disgustedly and brush them off, then I snatch one between my fingers and hold it to my computer's camera.

"Computer," I ask it. "What are these bugs? Should I be worried?"

The computer takes a second to analyze. "This appears to be a juju beetle. According to the most current research, juju beetles are entirely harmless—"

"Good."

"—unless they lay their eggs in open wounds or sores. Then the host will experience sharp, searing pains, followed by dizziness, fatigue, and in some cases, hallucinations."

I crush the juju beetle between my fingers. Idiot! I knew I should have bandaged up the wound instead of leaving it out in the open like that. I also shouldn't have left a two-inch slit in the tent door before I fell asleep. I bet these juju beetles have been crawling on me for hours. I've probably got loads of eggs buried in my thigh.

"Excellent. Amazing." I huff. "Well, they definitely planted their eggs in me. When will I start feeling the effects?"

"Effects typically begin eight to ten Earth hours after the eggs are planted."

"Fatal?"

"Negative. But highly unpleasant."

I triple-tap the collapse button on the tent and scoot outside before it packs itself. I have to release my tourniquet slowly to prevent reperfusion injuries—especially with those eggs inside me. So now I have lots of time to think.

My mind drifts to the other freedom fighters and where they might be. We were boarded by the enemy so quickly. I didn't have the chance to say goodbye to some of my friends before we escaped. I hope even one of them manages to get our information to the United Galaxies Senate—especially if

I never manage to get off this planet, wherever it is.

Not a great train of thought. To distract myself, I ask, "Hey, computer, are a bunch of juju beetles going to burst out of my leg?"

"Negative," the computer says. "The eggs will break inside your closed wound, releasing non-lethal amounts of toxic amniotic fluid."

I chuckle a little. "There's an ancient Earth video about a lifeform that plants its egg inside a man and it bursts out of his stomach. I saw it when I was in the academy. I figured maybe if the same thing happened to me, someone might make a video about me, too."

No response. Don't expect computers to joke with you.

After a couple hours, I finally get up. Yesterday's wound lights up like threads of fire and my head gets light. Everything starts to get a little blurry. Those dying juju beetle eggs are doing their work on me. Every left step sends hot pain through my thigh, and as time wears on, it gets heavier.

And I haven't even started climbing the mountain yet. At least I'm not hallucinating.

Sweat coats my face and chest. My canteen is nearly empty. And I haven't found a stream to refill it with.

The ground starts to slope. I'm moving upward. I do another Terrain Scan to get a full view of the mountain, and it looks good. The trees begin to thin out and I'm getting more sunshine between the gaps in the leafs.

I'm limping like an old man as the slope increases, and as I go, the ground appears to shift and rise, but I don't feel it. I blink hard. That puts the ground back to normal.

Great. The hallucinations are starting.

Before long, I reach a twenty-foot sheer cliff. I look to the left, then to the right. It seems to go all the way around the small mountain as far as I can see.

The ground shifts and dips again—but no, it doesn't. It's just my eyes playing tricks on me. I put my hand on the cliff face to steady myself, and it's absolutely solid. "Hey, computer, does this cliff go all the way around the mountain?"

"Affirmative."

"So I'm not just seeing things," I grumble. "How would you recommend I scale this thing? Do I even have enough rope?"

"The cliff face is an average of 14.18 meters high. You have ten meters of rope. That will make a climb impossible in most areas."

"You don't say."

"There is an area 201.67 meters to your right that is only 12.18 meters tall. If you are able to secure a rope at the top, you may be able to scale the cliff."

Seems as good of an idea as any. I trace the edge of the mountain, walking with the slope and being careful not to put too much weight on my bad leg. I'm sweating so hard that it's getting in my eyes. I wipe the salty liquid with my finger and put it on my tongue.

I tread forward cautiously, looking all around. By the time I reach the proper area, I look up and scowl. This is where my pocket computer told me to go. But from what I can see, the cliff face has to be more than fifty meters high. There's no way I can climb it.

I aim the computer at it. "You mean to tell me *this* is only twelve meters?"

"Negative. It is 12.18 meters."

"Well it's definitely *not*. It's gotta be five times that high!"

"My sensors indicate that it is 12.18 meters from where you stand. It is possible that you are hallucinating."

I scowl at the thing as if it can see me. "Well, I am

definitely hallucinating. But *you* might be malfunctioning, too. After all, your date is off."

"Allow me to run a brief self-diagnostic." It's silent for a moment. "Diagnostic complete. All systems and operations are functioning properly."

I shake my head. "Yeah, you things always think that. Nothing is ever your fault. Just like my ex." I let out a loud sigh. "You're *sure* that thing is only twelve meters?"

"Negative. It is 12.18 meters."

I purse my lips. "Well, I guess I'm going to trust you. If I die, it's your fault."

I tie the end of my rope into a lasso and fling it up. As I look up, the mountain and ground are tilting around me—I know it's just in my head, but it makes it hard to aim. The remnants of an old tree are sticking out of the cliff face, and a thick branch looks strong enough to carry my weight. It takes several tries, but I get it. Problem is, the end of the rope is now three feet over my head. I'll need something to give me a boost.

I'm looking around. Nothing big enough. The only thing I can think of is running up the wall like a ninja and grabbing the rope. And that's going to be nearly impossible with my bum leg.

But again, what other choice do I have? Mind over matter, right?

I take a few deep breaths to hype myself up, imagining myself as an Intergalactic Olympic competitor. Then I run toward the cliff face. My bad leg screams with every step. My eyes water and my thigh lights up, but I push on. I leap up the wall, take two steps, and jump backward, hand outstretched.

Success. I nab the very end of the rope and hold it tight. It drops a little bit as the lasso tightens around the branch. I nearly lose my grip but manage to hold on and painfully hoist myself up. It was nice having weight off my leg for a minute, but man, when did my arms get so weak? It was only a few days ago that I was doing exercises with the other freedom fighters. This rope should have been a breeze, even in my current state.

When I'm in the tree, I take a minute to catch my breath. I'm looking at the cliff face, but from what I can see, I'm not even halfway up. It's still insurmountably tall. I pull out my pocket computer to yell at it some more.

"Are you seeing this?" I point the camera at the cliff face. "I've still got like thirty meters to go!"

"Negative," the computer replies, "you only have 2.4 meters to go."

The tree suddenly droops, but it's just in my eyes. I don't feel it at all. Regardless, it startles me so badly I nearly fall out. I hold tight to a branch.

"Okay, computer, since you're so smart, exactly how do you expect me to climb the rest of the way?"

"Near the tree's trunk, 2.4 meters up and 1.2 meters to your right, you will find the lip of the cliff. From there, you can climb."

The color drains from my face. "So you're telling me I need to jump *away* from the tree and grab a ledge that I can't even see?"

"Affirmative."

"If you're wrong, I'll die."

"That may very well be correct if you fail to grasp the ledge."

I'm exhausted. I squint at the cliff. Is it another hallucination? Am I really going to put my life in the hands of this little machine in my pocket?

I act before I have too much time to mull it over. If I can't send out this beacon to get rescued, I'm dead anyway.

So we're going for it.

I put away the computer, cinch up my emergency pack, plant my feet, and jump.

O ANGEL, THOU HAST FALLEN!

"Will you be well enough for this mission, Herald Locken?"

Locken had been staring absently ahead, his fingers pressed together, drifting between prayer and absentmindedness. As the carriage jostled and bumped, the four Heralds inside spoke little. Their blue robes fell from their necks to their ankles, and they sat with perfect posture. All of them except Locken, at least. The knot in his chest made his posture and afterthought.

Herald Gwenli—a Herald from the Eighth Realm—had asked him the question. Her skin was darker than the other three Heralds, turned golden brown by the desert sun. Her sharp, dark eyes remained focused on Locken, waiting for an answer. Locken couldn't bring himself to make eye contact. He coughed and said, "The Council commands it, so it must be done."

The other two Heralds sat across from Locken and Gwenli. One was pale-skinned, all hair from his body completely shaved, including on his head, face, and arms. His name was Hal, a eunuch of the Ninth Realm, where they sterilize themselves soon after reproduction. They believe this practice tempers their desires and makes them more docile—less likely to wage war.

The other Herald, Troan, was the opposite—a strong, burly man with arms like tree trunks and a beard that reached the full length of his chest. He represented the First Realm. He focused on Locken with eyes like the sea, deep and wild, but tamed through years of meditation and discipline.

Herald Troan spoke with a voice like a lion. "He has trained many Heralds over the years. I would not be surprised if he has pulled some with him, based on our reports. His reputation will make this quite the scandal if it reaches the other Realms."

"Which makes his apostasy all the more puzzling," Herald Hal said. His voice was nearly as smooth as his head. "When I began the ministry, I longed to be tutored by Herald Xilon. The news of his recent deeds are shocking."

Locken was barely listening. His mind was elsewhere—recounting memories of studying under Xilon. Years studying under the decorated Herald, pouring over ancient books and serving the community in the name of the Gods. Those memories became tarnished when the Grand Council sent Locken on this mission. Xilon had been like a father to Locken for years—and now there are rumors of apostasy? It couldn't be true.

At least, Locken hoped they weren't.

The silence continued for several more minutes until Gwenli looked out the window. "We're here."

The words tightened a knot in Locken's stomach. The carriage lurched to a stop. Before the driver could come around and unlock the doors, Hal spoke.

"Fellow Heralds," the eunuch said. "Let us unite in

reciting the Herald's Creed. It will give us strength."

No one argued. They held each other's hands, making a tight circle in the cramped carriage. In unison, they said: "I will sow light, life, and knowledge in all that I do. I will never place my wisdom above the Gods. I will tame all carnal desires. I will refuse all unnecessary possessions. I will serve the downtrodden and the oppressed. And I will only sow death when there is no other choice."

When they let go, Hal kept holding on to Locken's hand. The eunuch looked directly into Locken's face, silently forcing him to make eye contact. "Take courage, friend. I know you will perform your duty with honor."

Locken forced a smile, but his mouth was dry and the emptiness inside him grew shockingly vast.

The carriage driver opened the door, and the Heralds stepped out. The other three Heralds stood in awe at the Capitol Cathedral, with its tall spires and stained-glass windows. A wide courtyard was encased in artfully crafted gates with the same trees, shrubbery, and flowers that Locken remembered from years ago.

The four Heralds marched through the gates. They felt the sharp stares of the gatekeepers follow them, and it was the same for all the others in the courtyard. All those on the Cathedral grounds were Heralds in training, but none of them wore the blue robes assigned by the Grand Council. This was new—against tradition.

More junior Heralds stood at the Cathedral doors, glaring at the unwanted visitors. They made no move, even when they were supposed to open the doors out of respect for their seniors.

Troan took a step forward. "Open the doors, Heralds. If you still answer to the Gods, you will let us perform our duty."

"We answer to the Gods," one said defiantly. "But not the Grand Council. Master Xilon has spoken."

Master Xilon? Not Herald Xilon? Locken frowned. *He's given himself a new title.*

"Then we ask you to let us enter as guests," Hal said gently. "We seek no harm or offense. Let us speak to him. We are all striving to serve the Gods. We are brothers and sisters under Heavenspire."

The junior Heralds looked at each other. Then one said, "Fine. Kreel will certainly have words for you. But if you try anything, you'll be met by the force of House Oakenwhit. And when you leave, you will not be welcome again. Go."

Locken's frown deepened. *The great Houses shouldn't have any jurisdiction over church matters. And Kreel isn't a name I know.*

The junior Heralds cautiously opened the double doors. The four Heralds entered the Cathedral and the doors slammed behind them.

Inside, their footsteps echoed off the ageless stone walls. The stained-glass windows threw multi-colored light along the floor. Rows of pews faced the front, where a podium was erected. Locken couldn't count how many sermons he had seen from that podium—he even gave some himself many years ago.

But there were two strange additions to the timeless Cathedral. One was the guards. Guards were stationed throughout the hall, standing at attention, garbed in armor representing House Oakenwhit. Locken glared at them as he passed. It appeared the powers of religion and state were no longer separate in the Second Realm. This had to be to House Oakenwhit's advantage.

The second addition was the gold. Statues, trinkets, fine furniture. The Cathedral was long supposed to be a place of godly beauty crafted in a spirit of modesty. Now the seeds of decadence had been sown. The interior was beginning to resemble one of the great Houses instead of a Cathedral of the Gods.

This was exemplified by the tall, ornate chair placed in front of the podium. Xilon sat in it. He was handsome and strong for an elderly man, with wavy silver hair combed back. His deep gray eyes pierced the visitors. Both his hands gripped the armrests, looking more like a king in a throne than a Herald in a Cathedral.

There was also a man who stood to his right. Like the soldiers, he was garbed in the colors of House Oakenwhit, but his outfit was vastly more ornate with gold trim and encrusted jewels. A sword dangled on his left hip, and his hand was perched on its hilt. His facial features resembled a hawk's, and he glowered at the visiting Heralds.

He stepped forward as the Heralds approached, making a barrier between them and Xilon.

"Your presence is *not* welcome here," he said, hand still on his sword. "The Grand Council's corruption is no longer an influence on the Second Realm."

"Perhaps you'll consider vacating the Cathedral, then," Gwenli said coolly. "It belongs, after all, to the Grand Council and the Heralds of Heavenspire. If Xilon no longer represents us, then he must leave. Your presence was never welcome here to begin with."

The man sneered. "I was invited. You speak bold words, woman. I suggest you watch your tongue."

Locken glanced at the guards poised throughout the hall. All their hands were on their weapons—swords, spears, bows and arrows. Locken's hands flexed and he controlled his breathing, readying himself for magic if necessary.

"Peace, Kreel," Xilon's voice was tender but strong. "Let me speak with my friends. I'm sure they'll see reason."

Kreel took his hand off his sword and stepped back to Xilon's side. Xilon motioned to the pews on the front row. "Please," he said. "Sit down."

"We'll remain standing," Troan said firmly. "You must come with us after all. Your trial awaits."

Xilon put his attention on Locken. "Good to see you again, Herald Locken. I've missed you dearly."

Locken's tone betrayed his sadness. "I wish our reunion were under different circumstances."

"Indeed." Xilon breathed deep and closed his eyes, as if uttering a silent prayer. "Your intentions are pure. You are all most honorable Heralds of Heavenspire. You serve the Gods faithfully. But, of a truth, the Grand Council has been marred by corruption for years. That is why I have seceded from its ranks."

"Its ranks?" Gwenli said. "You were never among the Grand Council. You were *denied* a position. For good reason, from what we were told."

Xilon's face pressed into a scowl. "Whatever that reason may be was never made known to me. But I assure you, I am still very much in the service of the Gods. The Grand Council is a cancer that I have removed from my service. That is the beginning and end of it."

"What's all this, then?" Troan motioned to all the fine things. "*Refuse all unnecessary possessions. Tame carnal desires.* You've let this Cathedral become a house of excess. You've abandoned the Herald's Creed."

Kreel smirked horribly. "House Oakenwhit insisted upon these gifts in honor of our new agreement. Master Xilon did not seek these things. His heart remains pure and tame. Yours, however… seems a tad wild."

Troan glared at Kreel and took a threatening step forward. Hal threw out an arm to restrain him, and Kreel chuckled at the sight.

"Please, please listen," Xilon said. He got up from his seat and clasped his hands behind his back. "I'll admit that I desired a seat on the Grand Council for years. I felt I deserved it, given my decades of service to the Gods. But the Grand Council saw things differently. I was heartbroken. I wondered how my service was still insufficient. That's when I was approached by my friends at House Oakenwhit. And they provided me with damning evidence of the Council's corruption. The news shattered me. I felt the very foundation of my identity shattered and broken. But I knew I must separate myself from among them to remain pure. And truthfully, I feel more connected to the Gods than ever before."

Locken blinked and frowned. "You keep speaking of this corruption. What is it?"

Kreel was the one who answered. "Interfering with political matters across all Ten Realms. The Grand Council of Heavenspire swears neutrality, but throughout history, they have orchestrated coups, wars, and trade for their personal gain. They are no better than the great Houses. I'm not surprised you haven't heard. They're not keen on sharing this side of their history."

The Heralds tensed at the accusation. But Hal shook his head. "These accusations have reached my ears before. Baseless. Brittle rumors. Herald Xilon, surely you don't believe this worm. House Oakenwhit clearly seeks to exploit your influence."

"They cannot accept the truth," Kreel murmured with pity. There was also a touch of venom in his tone.

"With House Oakenwhit's sponsorship," Xilon said, "my pupils and I can serve the Gods in peace. The people of the Second Realm will no longer feel obligated to donate to our operations. This is what's best for all of us. House Oakenwhit hasn't pushed or prodded me in any way."

Gwenli raised an eyebrow and looked all around. "Yet, this holy place is full of its soldiers."

Taking courage, Locken stepped forward. He stared deeply into Kreel's eyes, reading him. He summoned the magic from a reservoir in his body, feeling for the gift of discernment, trying to find a truth that was buried.

"What is House Oakenwhit planning?" Locken asked softly and directly. "The House must have great and unpopular plans if you're buying the support of a beloved Herald. What are they?"

Kreel's expression turned dark. His hand went back to his sword. "You know nothing of which you speak."

There is a buried truth here. The magic confirmed it. Locken said, "You are a snake in the grass, waiting to strike. My master, a respected man across the Ten Realms, is nothing but a pawn in your political game, isn't he?"

Shing! Kreel drew his sword and swept forward. The blade's tip pointed just inches from Locken's throat. But Locken didn't move.

"Know your place, Herald," Kreel threatened. "I will not be insulted again."

There is a truth buried here. The magic confirmed it stronger and louder.

"Kreel!" Xilon pleaded. "Sheath your weapon!"

"You see what's happening, don't you Master?" Kreel said. "The Council sees you as a threat. They've sent these Heralds to abduct you on the guise of a trial. But you and I know you'll never leave that trial alive. We see through their web of lies."

"The only liar here is you, Kreel," Locken said. "You've desecrated this place of worship and made it an extension of

House Oakenwhit. You are commanded to leave."

Kreel sneered and tsked. "Or what?"

Locken spoke the answer with his eyes—a dreadful promise and a warning. Kreel got the message, because he scoffed again, then slid his sword into its scabbard. He stood by Xilon, then gave a tight, shrill whistle.

The tension in the room spiked. Soldiers shouted and held breaths released as arrows left their bows. The Heralds' training had made them quick. As the arrows fell, the Heralds threw magical shields. But they couldn't guard themselves from all angles. Arrows pierced their legs and arms. Troan took shafts to the stomach and chest. He moaned as he collapsed to the floor, blood seeping around his body.

Xilon leapt from his chair. "*What are you doing?*"

"What is necessary, Master!" Kreel said as he ripped his sword free.

"*Cease this now!*" Xilon bellowed.

The soldiers converged, defying Xilon's orders. As the Heralds healed themselves, pushing magic through their bodies, they retaliated. Hal threw his hands like a windmill, flinging the long wooden pews through the air, toppling over soldiers. The screams and clashing armor echoed in the cavernous hall. Gwenli tore her own sword from a sheath on her side, then cast a spell to make her skin hard as iron. With that, she advanced on a band of soldiers, ready to deal a deadly dance.

Locken focused on Kreel. Sparks and flames leapt from his fingertips, and he bent his knees. "You've murdered a Herald of Heavenspire this day. Your life is required as payment."

"Murderers and hypocrites, all of you," Kreel said with narrowed eyes.

The doors flew open. More soldiers poured in. With

more precise movements, Hal magically threw more pews across the hall, knocking aside soldiers. Some died and some were broken. For the Heralds, the final sentence of the Herald's Creed roared in their ears—*only sow death when there is no other choice.*

Gwenli had suffered many wounds to the legs, arms, and face, but bloody bodies scattered around her. Her wounds stitched quickly as she pushed the magic through her bones and muscles, but it wouldn't hold for too long. Forces kept flooding in.

"Seal the doors!" she cried.

Hal responded by throwing four pews against the double doors. They slammed shut, filling the hall with a resounding *boom.* There were no more entering forces, but the Cathedral was still filled with dozens of soldiers screaming for murder.

Meanwhile, Locken and Kreel remained in a standoff—Locken with his magic, and Kreel with his blade.

"Please, Kreel! Stop this!" Xilon begged. "Look what you've done!"

Kreel ignored him, never looking away from Locken. "You won't strike until I strike you. Then you can claim it's self-defense."

"I'm fully justified to set you ablaze right now," Locken replied icily. "I won't strike because I serve the Gods. You won't strike because you're a coward."

Kreel's smirk dropped. Baring his teeth, he swung. Locken ducked. Another swing. Another dodge. Finding an opening, Locken blasted a bolt of electricity at Kreel. But the bolt was absorbed by an amulet Kreel wore around his neck. The dark blue stone glowed and faded as it sucked up the blast.

A Darkmage Amulet! Locken marveled and cursed himself for not noticing it earlier. At the sight of it, Locken knew all of his magic would be ineffective against Kreel. In this state, he was essentially defenseless.

Locken cast his eyes about. Gwenli had fallen, but not without all the soldiers around her. Hal had also bested all the soldiers battling him, but he was mortally wounded. He sat with his back against a remaining pew, blood seeping onto his robe. His face was pale and he breathed with labor, but he saw Locken's situation. With one final spell, he stretched out his hand and flung Gwenli's sword toward Locken. Locken snatched it from the air and brandished it. And with that, Hal collapsed.

The stench of death filled Locken's nose and the air grew still. Kreel stood close, his weapon raised.

"And then there were three!" Kreel mused. "But you won't last long. I've trained with the blade my entire life."

"*Stop this!*" Xilon shouted. "*In the name of the Gods!*"

Kreel didn't listen. "You'll meet your friends soon, Herald. May the Gods give you justice!" Kreel lifted his weapon, but he gasped and his eyes turned wide. The sword fell from his limp hand, clanging onto the floor. His body followed, collapsing into a heap.

Xilon was left holding a dagger in mid-air, its tip red and wet. He dropped it next to Kreel's body and he slumped into his seat. He looked like a man of his proper age now, tired, hunched, and aghast.

Heart still thrashing and mind racing, Locken dropped Gwenli's sword. He fell to his knees, staring at the floor, numb as the fallen bodies grew pale and stiff around him. Just a few feet away, Xilon let a similar feeling wash over him.

Silence swallowed them. Then Xilon said mournfully, "It was never meant to come to this."

Locken said nothing.

"This is all my doing," Xilon despaired. "All I wanted was

to serve the Gods. But look. Look at this symphony of death. Three Heralds. Countless soldiers. An advisor to a noble House. Surely the Gods will smite me for this. I fear…" The next words took effort. "I fear my damnation is secure."

Locken found his tongue. "There must be justice for today. The Grand Council will demand it."

"You know I no longer answer to them."

Another long silence. Then Locken said, "But you must make recompense with the Gods. Somehow."

Xilon gave Locken a look that Locken had rarely seen before—submission. He was no longer a master. He was a tired man, stricken spiritually and physically, waiting to hear his fate.

"I will not answer to the Grand Council," Xilon said. "But I will answer to *you*, Herald Locken. Your heart is pure. Your mind is sharp. I know, in this holy Cathedral, on this day, you can exact on me a sentence that will please the Gods. I know it. So please." He paused. "Please."

Locken's heart lurched. The weight his old master had just laid on him was astonishing. But as Xilon said the words, a flutter of peace fell upon his spirit. *Yes, he was right.* Locken felt the Gods' blessing.

After a brief, silent prayer, Locken opened up the doors of heavenly inspiration. The answer came swiftly and surely. The words that followed were hardly his own.

"Herald Xilon," he said, trying to keep his voice steady. "You are hereby sentenced to exile. Separate yourself from the civilized world. With me, Herald Locken, as holy witness, you must swear to never know another face or voice for the rest of your days. And there, you must strive to make peace with the Gods. Do you accept this fate, Herald Xilon?"

Xilon's eyes shone with pain and pride. He nodded faintly. "I swear it." He forced a feeble smile. "Of all the voices and faces I saw before my exile, I'm glad it was yours. I love you, my boy. And I know you love me, too. Despite it all."

Locken's eyes stung. He swallowed and cleared his throat. "I believe the Council will accept this. May the Gods be with you, Herald Xilon. I pray you'll find peace and forgiveness."

They stood for a prolonged moment, wanting to hold on, to keep this moment for all that they could. But at last, they knew there was nothing more to be said. Xilon gave a subtle nod, then vanished. Locken did the same. He reappeared by the carriage outside the Cathedral doors. He jumped inside and commanded the driver to flee with haste.

GOD ONLY KNOWS

I had just graduated from college and was working my first full-time job when I saw a billboard for Brian Wilson performing in my home town. As soon as I parked my car, I texted you to tell you he was coming through. You grew up with the Beach Boys and I had gained an appreciation for Brian Wilson's musical genius, so I told you we should go together. You told me you'd take care of it.

You got us front-row tickets. Front-row tickets to see a living legend. And I'd get to see that living legend with you.

I put on a nice shirt befitting the California sun, and we went to the theater. You were strong enough to make it all the way down those steps back then. With our seats, we were just twenty feet away from one of the greatest artists in the history of rock and pop.

Brian had lost a step with age, but that was okay. He made it a point to play "God Only Knows" without assistance. His chords touched every corner of my heart as I listened to him play that song that came from the deepest wells of his soul. When he was done, you leaned toward me and whispered that he didn't play like he used to. That's when you saw the tears in my eyes.

I didn't care that Brian Wilson wasn't as polished as he was in the sixties. He was *here*, playing his masterpiece decades later, giving it his all despite his limitations. And that made the song just as beautiful, if not more so.

You're the same now. You struggle to walk and stand. You spend most days in your chair drifting in and out of sleep. But that doesn't change the fact that I've always been your little boy trying to make you proud. You've always been Brian Wilson performing on that stage to me.

And God only knows what I'd be without you.

HOLLY'S CORNER

Maribel fought back her tears. "I'm sure you heard the news."

Her one employee, Taylor, pursed their lips and nodded. With bright pink hair, overalls, and an assortment of colorful buttons, Taylor looked like they should be anything but miserable.

"We're running out of money," Maribel forced herself to say. "And we've held out for as long as we can. But by the end of this week, we won't have money to pay you."

Taylor swallowed and sniffled. "I understand, Mrs. McFadden. I'm sorry."

Maribel held out her arms and Taylor came in for a hug. They held each other for a long while. Taylor kept sniffling into Maribel's shoulder, making her sweater wet with tears.

"I'm the one who's sorry," Maribel said as she patted Taylor's back. "You've been a joy to work with these past six years. I wish there was more we could do."

Taylor withdrew and wiped their eyes with their sleeve. They managed to say, "What will you and Todd do?"

"We don't know yet," Maribel said. "This store has been twenty years of our lives. But we'll manage. Don't worry about us."

"Let me know what I can do to help."

"You're very kind, Taylor. Thank you."

With that, Taylor gave Maribel one more hug, then walked out the door. As usual, the door didn't close all the way—Maribel had to push it. When she did, she turned around and leaned her back against it. She stared at the floor and sniffled for a good while, gazing around the store she had owned for two decades.

Holly's Corner. A humble collective of used paperbacks stuffed into thrifted bookcases spread around a room. The display table at the front had folded cardboard under one leg to keep it from wobbling. The carpet had never been replaced, and the musty smell made it obvious. And if you went near the back wall, you could hear the sink in the employee bathroom leaking.

Maribel didn't take her back off the front door. Why bother? It's not like a customer would come walking in. They only saw a handful every day.

While Maribel was in her despair, Todd limped into the room. He took the spot at the front counter, ran his fingers through his graying hair, and let out a great sigh. He looked at Maribel with soft blue eyes and said, "You talked to Taylor?"

Maribel nodded.

"How did they take it?"

She shrugged. "As well as they could have."

Todd's shoulders drooped. "It's a damn shame. They were saving up to fix their car, too."

Maribel paused and asked her husband, "How are you?"

Todd shook his head defeatedly. "As good as I can hope. I've been thinking about her a lot today."

"Holly?"

"Yeah," Todd said. "She would be thirty-four... thirty-five now. Maybe have kids of her own." A quiet, thoughtful moment. "We did a good thing here, 'Bel. I tried to talk you out of it years ago, but you were right."

That brought half a smile to Maribel's face. "Can I talk you into posting on social media while I print flyers?"

Todd rolled his eyes and slid behind the computer. "If there's anything I *won't* miss, it's posting on social media."

That made Maribel laugh a little, despite it all.

"GOING OUT OF BUSINESS. THANK YOU FOR TWENTY WONDERFUL YEARS. ALL BOOKS 50% OFF. ALL SALES ARE FINAL."

That's what the flyer said. Maribel posted them all around the store and stapled them to posts up and down the street. She even called the local newspaper to get it placed in print. It was a small enough town and everyone knew everyone, so Milo over at the *Daily Star* offered to place it pro bono. He expressed how sad he was that the place was closing down. Maribel thanked him profusely but inwardly grumbled because she never saw Milo at the store even once.

Thankfully, customers poured in—at least more than usual. Folks they only saw at church or Rotary Club came in to buy armfuls of paperbacks. The conversations were all the same. "I'm so sorry the place is closing down. Holly's Corner has been a staple of our community. We'll miss having our little book shop on Main Street."

It was like that for weeks. Maribel put on a good face and tried to stay strong, but the countdown to closing day felt like a weight steadily dropping in her chest. Decades of work was coming to a sputtering, disappointing end.

The last day of Holly's Corner was its biggest in years. Hundreds of books got sold, but there was still a lot of inventory left. For the next week, Todd and Maribel boxed them up and labeled them for schools, libraries, and thrift stores. They sold all the bookcases and furniture for pennies on the dollar.

They even uprooted the front counter. That was one of the hardest parts. Maribel remembered Todd building that front counter board by board back when he was stronger and his leg wasn't bad. He kept that counter beautifully kept for years. But now, it was scrap lumber. All but one part.

"Wait!" Maribel said when two men came over to dismantle it. She pointed at a spot right below where the computer used to be. "That part. Can you pull it off? I don't want that to be scrap."

One of the men said it would be no problem. He grabbed a hammer and carefully leveraged a decorative board away from the counter. It was a sign—barely as long as Maribel's arm and only six inches tall. It was a plaque baring the bookstore's name, *Holly's Corner*—carved, sanded, and stained to perfection.

But that was the last of it. The carpenters hauled away the fragments of once-carefully crafted wood. In the end, Maribel and Todd were left with a large, empty room with musty carpet and blank walls. Maribel couldn't help it—her shoulders trembled and the tears burst forth. She tightly hugged the Holly's Corner sign, dreading the moment when they would walk out for the last time. Todd put his arm around her, rubbing her shoulder with his thumb.

When the tears dried, they gathered their courage and hauled the remaining boxes into Todd's rickety old sedan. The car churned and started. They drove away, leaving behind the vacant room that was once the town's only bookstore.

For a few minutes, they were silent. Nothing but the car's dull rumble filled their ears. Every pothole made the struts squeak. They didn't even listen to the radio—Todd and Maribel just simmered in the silence.

Finally, Todd spoke. "Do you remember when you first brought up the idea of opening a bookstore?"

Maribel nodded. "It wasn't long after Holly passed."

"What did I say?"

"I don't remember. It was so long ago."

"I'll tell you," Todd said. "I said that we shouldn't take on another burden after we had just lost our only child. I said a bookstore would be too much to take care of when we were already going through so much."

"You were right," Maribel said.

"I was," Todd said. "But it was worth it."

A lump formed in Maribel's throat. She didn't look at Todd, because she knew if she did, she'd start sobbing again.

"It never stopped being hard, 'Bel," he said. "We knew there was no money in book selling. But my gosh… we watched kids grow up in there. Remember little Mikey Alton? Came in to get a picture book when he was in first grade? Then we sold him those manga books before he went to college last summer? I swear he was in that store every day. Then there were the poetry nights, and the book club meetings, even the AA meetings on Wednesday… We made a place for the community, 'Bel. If we got to do it all over again, I'd do it in a heartbeat. No question."

Maribel swallowed down her emotions and brought herself to speak. "Holly would have loved that place, too."

Todd paused as he gathered his feelings. Maribel knew he was trying not to cry—he always got quiet like this when he did.

"Yes," he said. "She would have." Another pause. "Part of me was hoping we'd see some miracle—that a check would magically appear in the mail and the store would be saved.

But no. Sometimes… Sometimes things just end. And that's okay. We had something special for a long while, 'Bel, and I'm grateful."

They pulled into the driveway, stopped the car, and turned off the lights. When the car went still, Maribel squeezed Todd's hand while it was still on the gear shifter. "I love you, Todd. Thanks for this adventure."

Todd smiled. "I love you, too. It was my pleasure."

They hauled the boxes into the house, pushing them into a corner of the living room to worry about them another day. The last thing Maribel brought in was the Holly's Corner sign —the one stripped from the front counter. She kept hugging it like a child as she moved down the hallway.

She opened the last door to the left—Holly's bedroom.

It was a fourteen-year-old girls' room frozen in time— marked by the most popular things of twenty years ago. There were posters on the wall of at least three boy bands. Stuffed animals congregated on a bed that had been perfectly made for years. The dresser was overflowing with makeup, necklaces, and earrings.

Near the foot of the bed was a bookcase stuffed with colorful paperbacks. There were novels about cute vampire boys and warrior princesses. Most of them had been untouched for decades. The very top of the bookcase was empty, though, which was perfect. Maribel took the Holly's Corner sign and set it there. She adjusted it until it leaned against the wall just right.

This would be Holly's Corner now. But if she was being honest, the store was always Holly's. It was always for her.

She stroked the bedspread as she walked out. When she turned off the light, she almost thought she saw her little girl laying there, curled up with a book like she always was. Maribel knew it was a mirage, but it was these moments that unexpectedly struck her with sweetness and pain. Tonight, she would hold to the sweet part.

THE BEACON AND THE WOLF, PART 2

This feeling—in the air, arms outstretched, heart pounding in my ears—is one of the most equally exhilarating and terrifying things I've ever felt. The second it's there feels like a lifetime. It looks like my hands are headed for solid rock. I'm going to die here—alone, broken, and lost.

But then my hands go *through* the cliff. And almost immediately, the hallucination evaporates. I'm hanging from the cliff. My elbows and forearms have found flat ground. I cackle out of relief. My feet struggle below me, but I manage to pull myself up and roll onto the surface.

I lay there, face up, breathing hard for a long moment. With my eyes closed against the sun, I pull out the pocket computer.

"I owe you an apology," I tell it.

"No apology is necessary."

That puts another thought in my head. This pocket computer has been right about mostly everything since I landed here. So is it possible that I really am… five years in the future? Was I stuck in cryosleep for that long? That can't be true. The tubes weren't built to last that long. If that's the case, the information I carry would be long expired and I would have no reason to be rescued anyway.

Before I follow the end of that thought, I have another one: these hallucinations might kill me if I let them persist. And I have an idea to get them over with sooner. Supposedly, the eggs inside my leg break, release the toxins, and cause the hallucinations. There are probably still some in my leg that haven't broken yet. Maybe if I can force them to…

I scoot away from the edge, sit up, and start punching my thigh with all my strength. Oh man, I hope I never feel pain like that again. I can feel those tiny juju beetle eggs breaking, popping like little pimples under my skin. The cuts feel like lava, and that lava spreads through the rest of that leg and up into my abdomen. I turn over and vomit. Hard.

As the bile pools around the grass by my face, my head starts to feel more normal. My body is filthy from dried sweat, but I no longer feel the lightheadedness that's plagued me all day.

I am, however, totally drained. I crawl farther away from the edge—farther away from my puke—and lay down for what has to be an hour. My mouth is dry. My lips are cracking. Throwing up robbed me of a lot of fluids, and now I'm *very* dehydrated. And out of water.

"It's better than seeing things that aren't there," I tell myself through a dry throat. Then I force myself to get up and move.

Thankfully, the walk to the top of the mountain isn't nearly as treacherous. There's a steady incline. The trees are getting farther apart. I'm dragging hard from the lack of water and my bum leg, but with any luck, a ship can rescue me in less than a day after I send the distress signal.

It's late afternoon (I think) by the time I reach the top. It's a nice, flat plateau that has to be about a quarter mile in diameter. And the best part? There are barely any trees. I can see loads of trees on the surface in every direction, though. I'm nearly level with them, so they spread out like a vast, green carpet. Hopefully the beacon can get a decent signal up here, otherwise I'm a goner.

Slowly, weakly, I pull it from my pack. Set it up. Lick my parched lips. Point it to the sky. Press the button.

It whirs and powers up. Then it stops and gives three error beeps.

"Poor conditions," it says. "Please select alternative location."

My heart drops into my stomach. What? That can't be right! What else could it possibly be?

I pick it up and move it about a hundred meters closer to the plateau's center. Same process. But after it whirs up, I still get the same three beeps and error message. Poor conditions. Please select alternative location.

"Computer," I'm nearly shouting through a scratchy mouth. "What's actually messing with my emergency beacon?"

"Based on climate and terrain, there should not be anything obstructing the beacon's signal."

My eyes turn wide as I consider the possibility. "Could I have gotten a faulty… beacon?"

"The possibility is not zero."

My face turns hot and my hands shake. After all this time, thinking my pocket computer was the faulty one, it was my emergency beacon.

I'm stranded here. I'm going to die from starvation or thirst or whatever alien beast eats me first. And as far as I know, I'm not even in the same year I thought I was.

In my anger, I wind up my leg and kick the beacon. The

apparatus skips along the grass, eventually coming to a stop.

Then, on its own, it powers up. But I don't get an error message. Instead, I get a flashing green light. It's sending the beacon. It's working.

My legs give out and I sink to a sitting position. I stare at the beacon, laying on its side, finally working, and I'm not sure whether to laugh or cry.

"I can't wait to get off this rock," I mumble before I collapse.

Night approaches. I eat some of my rations and wash it down with a warm cup of piss. It's just as pleasant as you'd imagine. I manage to get some sleep in my tent, but I make sure my zipper is closed all the way so I don't get any unwanted visitors.

Night falls. I'm woken up by the sound of engines. There's a bright light outside. And my tent is flapping like a hurricane is passing through.

A rescue ship!

I scramble along my hands and feet and exit the tent. The tent blows away in the gust, but who cares? I'm saved! It's a small United Galaxies Armada ship that's landed just a hundred yards away from me—likely manned by five to six crewmen. These things can jump into and out of hyperspace easily—they're just big enough that the crewmen don't need cryotubes for hyperspace. They were probably passing by this weird planet when they got my signal.

The ship settles on the ground and the engines stop. A loud hiss sounds as the hydraulics lower and a hatch opens. From out of the hatch come five crewmen, all dressed in UGA uniforms.

It's hard to describe the relief I feel in this moment. Just yesterday, I thought I was going to die on this strange planet. Now, I've got five UGA crewmen to take me to safety.

But I'm still not in the clear. I need to figure out if these are freedom fighters or imperial sympathizers. The freedom fighters have a few key words that they use to differentiate their comrades. I'll try some out once I have the chance to talk to them.

Three of them approach me and two of them hang back. The two are carrying plasma rifles while the other three keep blasters similar to mine. As they get closer to me, their faces twist into veiled disgust. I'm sure I look like a disaster—sunburned, crack lips, wearing a jumpsuit that's half bloody with a shredded left leg. And let's not forget the dried puke on my collar.

"You look like you've been through it, friend!" one of them says. "We got your signal and dropped out of hyperspace for you. How long have you been waiting?"

I shrug. "Signal went up maybe eight or ten Earth hours ago. Been here for a couple of days. Do any of you have water?"

Another one of them hands a canteen to me. I drink deeply. It's the best sensation I've ever felt. When you're shriveled up from dehydration, it doesn't matter if water is ice cold or boiling hot. It's going to be the best thing you ever tasted. I stop to take a breath after several long swigs. "I'm glad you're here. This sitting duck needed to fly, but my wings are clipped."

That last sentence was the typical distress call among the freedom fighters. *This sitting duck needs to fly.* If there's another freedom fighter nearby, they'll reply with, *You just need to shake the water off.*

They look at me blankly for a second, then one of the officers responds to me as if suddenly struck by it. "Well, we found you! Looks like you just had some water to shake off."

Huh. Not exactly on the nose, but it's close enough. This

crew is probably one of ours. I stand up. "Good. What star date is it? My name is Private Gerald Figgins. I'm in possession of important intel regarding Admiral Garand's rise to power. If the date is right and I wasn't in cryosleep for too long, Admiral Garand is staging a coup against the United Galaxies Senate in less than sixty Earth days. I have a list of his associates, so we need to move fast."

They stare at me before exchanging glances. The one closest to me nods. "Right. Let's get you on the ship. There's no time to lose."

I start walking with them, but I'm surprised when two of them reach out and grab my arms. It doesn't feel friendly. I shoot them looks, but now they're ignoring me as they guide me onto the ship. The two soldiers hanging back with the plasma rifles eye me threateningly. Something in the pit of my stomach is protesting, and it's not my ration bars.

Then, something in the distance. A burning red light descending from the clouds. But it's not falling—it's going too fast for that. As I squint at it, I realize it's not a light. It's the red glow of thrusters. It shoots straight for the ground, then pulls parallel to the treetops.

I think it's coming for us.

"Captain, what is that?" the soldier next to me says.

A flash of blaster fire streaks by my head—and through *his*. The soldier releases my arm as he falls. When I look down, his face is blank, punctured with a round, smoking hole the size of my fist. I can see the cauterized brain matter inside.

"*It's the Iron Wolf!*" someone shouts.

Immediate panic. And they've put me in the middle of it all.

"Get the prisoner on board!" the captain says. "Open fire! Go, go, go!"

Prisoner? I'm a *prisoner* now? I'm dragged toward the hatch as everyone falls on their bellies and points their blasters toward the Iron Wolf. It's a barrage of shouts and commands as they send streaks of red across the dark sky, aimed at the assailant. But the assailant is still too far in the distance.

But *we're* not too far away for *them*, because one of the plasma rifle guys takes a thick bolt through the chest. He gargles and collapses. Someone screams his name. The plasma bolt would have taken off my leg if I were six inches away.

I'm dragged up the ship's loading ramp and dumped inside, then my captor points a blaster at me and commands, "Stay here!" He scrambles to the bottom of the loading ramp to scoop up the dead man's plasma rifle and open fires.

While they shout and scream, my eyes dart around the ship. My heart sinks. Near the cockpit are two identical red banners that go from ceiling to floor. They have an ancient Earth letter G on them, and Admiral Garand is printed looking powerful and stoic, facing the distance as if looking to the future.

These aren't freedom fighters. These are Garand's men—imperial soldiers.

I get to my knees and peer through the door. The screaming has slowed down. The men have been picked off one by one. Five smoking bodies are all strewn on the ground, limbs askew. The last one standing is the captain. He stands firm, shoulders back, chin up. He's facing what has to be the Iron Wolf. I don't know what I was expecting the Iron Wolf to be, but it wasn't *this*.

The Iron Wolf is a robot standing nearly seven feet tall. It's built like a steel gorilla, walking with thick, hulking steps. What's most surprising is that it has the small, flat head of a

Bebo unit—one of those basic robotic assistance units used for leisure ships and college campuses. Someone has retrofitted this one to high hell—nearly every limb has a weapon attached to it.

The Iron Wolf looks down on the captain. The captain throws up Garand's signature salute.

"Empire Forever!" he shouts. "Long live Emperor Garand! Death to the—"

He doesn't get to finish. The Iron Wolf picks him up and hurls him like a javelin. I hear his terrified scream echo into the distance as his body disappears behind the mountain's edge.

Then the Iron Wolf turns to me. I gasp and duck away. I fumble for my blaster with sweaty hands, wondering what good its remaining shots could be against the Iron Wolf. But soon, the Iron Wolf darkens the hatch. I sit up and point my blaster at it. The Wolf doesn't seem phased. Its head tilts, watching me like a curious dog.

"Hello," it says in a pleasant robotic voice. "I am Bebo. The threats have been neutralized. We are here to rescue you."

I blink a couple of times, still pointing my blaster. "We? Who's we?"

A couple of beeps from Bebo/Iron Wolf. "Captain Childs, the Imperials have been eliminated. It is safe to transport down."

Bebo steps aside just as two people materialize several yards away—they obviously have a Transportation deck on their ship, wherever it is. One of the people is a beautiful blonde woman in a captain's uniform. Her face is stern, obviously weathered by many battles. The other person is a strong, brown-haired woman garbed in black leather and carrying a plasma rifle.

The women march toward me with purpose. I don't point my blaster at them—probably not the best idea with the Iron Wolf present.

"You," the blonde captain says as she approaches. "You one of Garand's men? Or no?"

"Garand?" I say, frowning. "No way. I'm trying to *stop* Garand!"

The captain looks at Bebo. The robot says, "No deceit detected in his voice, captain."

"Good," the captain says. She turns her attention to me again. "I'm Victoria Childs, captain of the starship Dauntless. This is Kira, my first in command."

"The *Dauntless*?" I ask, my eyes wide. "I've heard stories about you guys! You're the stuff of legend! But wait… I thought Hugh Gosling was the captain of the Dauntless. You guys are with the freedom fighters?"

Captain Childs's smirk drops. She looks at Kira then back to me. "Tell us your story, stranger. Then you'll get ours."

So I do. I tell them about my last mission with the freedom fighters—obtaining information about Admiral Garand's plan to overthrow the United Galaxies Senate. Then I tell them about how my crew was attacked by Garand's men, how I escaped, and how I ended up here. They listen intently the entire time.

When it's their turn, I hear things I do *not* want to hear.

My pocket computer was never wrong—I was in cryosleep for five Earth years. Admiral Garand's coup was successful, and there is no more United Galaxies. Now it's Emperor Garand and the New Galactic Order. It's oppression and fear everywhere. Former United Galaxies leaders were imprisoned or executed if they didn't fall in line. Victoria Childs is now captain of the Dauntless because its famous former captain, Hugh Gosling, was killed in battle nearly two years ago. A lot of the original Dauntless crew is dead.

It all hits me like a tidal wave. I press my palms into my eyes. I failed. Our mission failed. My information could have prevented this, but instead, the United Galaxies fell while I was stuck in cryosleep on an alien planet.

Captain Childs squats down next to me and puts her hand on my shoulder. I don't uncover my face—I don't want her to see me crying. But my body still trembles with grief.

"We still need people in this fight," she says. "Things aren't hopeless. The Imperials thought they could squash the freedom fighters after the insurrection, but our numbers are growing. Even those close to Garand are starting to turn. We've acquired an informant inside the New Galactic Order —an officer of influence. I can't give you all the details now, but we're planting the seeds to take this whole thing down from the inside. It's dangerous. You might die. But it sounds like you were prepared for that anyway. So, you ready to get back to work, Private?"

I find the strength to pull my hands away. My eyes are red and puffy, but her words have lit a fire inside. Thinking of the friends I lost—the freedom lovers who have sacrificed their lives—I swallow, purse my lips, and nod. "Yes, Captain."

A smile. Then she stands up and gives me her hand. "Get up. We've got fascists to kill."

THE GRASS ON THE OTHER SIDE

He was Mary's client before he was her lover. A tall man with dark hair, graying at the edges, and a wide, even smile. Always perfectly tan. Always perfectly dressed. When Mary came over to clean the house, he would be with his wife, getting ready to leave so Mary could clean uninterrupted.

The rich man's wife would hardly ever look at Mary. It's not that the wife hated Mary, she just never thought of her. Mary was hardly more than a shadow to her—always there, but undeserving of attention.

Over time, the wife became less present. She would take frequent trips with her girlfriends, and each time, the husband would stay home while Mary did the cleaning. He tried to stay out of her way, but occasionally, he would hover around Mary and talk. The rich man's wife was so cold and distant, Mary wasn't terribly surprised that the rich man needed someone to talk to. He was probably very lonely.

He would speak slowly, using small words so Mary could understand. He was warm. Charming. Earned all of his money through investments after paying his way through college. Mary liked that. And he saw Mary as a businesswoman, not just the "help." Mary liked that even more.

Mary and the rich man became friends. That's when Mary became more than a shadow to the rich man's wife.

She started becoming critical of Mary's cleaning—commenting on areas she missed (which she hadn't), telling her to be better. After a few times, the husband defended Mary, saying the tub or the counter or the carpet looked fine. When he would, the wife would glare at him, silently threatening. That would silence him.

But the talks between Mary and the rich man continued when the wife was away. Then he asked Mary if he could take her to dinner. Just as friends.

Mary considered saying no—the tiny voice in her chest told her to. Mary had her own husband at home and knew he wouldn't approve. But he did so many things *she* didn't approve of: going to the bar with his friends while using *her* cleaning money, watching TV for hours instead of looking for work, sleeping the day away and giving her more to clean when she got home each night.

So, before she could reconsider it, she said yes.

It was Mary's first time at a five-star restaurant. She felt out of place there, like pimple on a supermodel's face. She wore her best dress and spent hours on her hair, but she still felt like an outcast among the upper class. The rich man didn't seem to mind. They dined on fine steaks and talked for hours. It was nice to talk without the distractions of scrubbing, too. The evening felt magical to Mary.

The rich man dropped Mary off a block away from home so his fancy car wouldn't look suspicious out front. He kissed Mary on the cheek before she stepped onto the sidewalk. He didn't ask for permission, but Mary didn't mind. It actually made her stomach leap. She couldn't remember the last time her husband made her feel that way.

When she got home, her husband was sitting on the couch watching a show. Mary froze, wondering if he would ask her where she was or why she looked so lovely. But he didn't. He didn't even look at her. So Mary went to the bedroom and fell asleep. Her husband didn't leave the couch to join her that night.

That became the first of many evenings. The rich man took Mary to plays, concerts, and more fine restaurants. It was rich people dates—not the typical bar dates or mini golf games Mary went on when she was single. The rich man made her feel like a prize. She felt adored for the first time in a long time.

What was worse, she felt herself falling in love with him.

Mary could tell the rich man's wife noticed. But instead of being cruel, she became more distant. The wife spent over a month away. The rich man said she was visiting family.

But Mary never saw her again.

The rich man's wife filed for divorce. She was never coming back. That weekend, the rich man paid Mary to help him box his wife's things instead of clean the house.

Mary asked him how he was feeling. He said well enough, he had been expecting it. Their marriage had never been truly happy and it had only gotten worse in recent years. Mary asked the rich man if if his wife had been unfaithful. He said he didn't know. But she suspected *him* of being unfaithful with Mary. Which wasn't true.

Even if Mary wanted it to be.

When Mary got home that weekend, her husband accused her of having an affair with the rich man. Mary denied it, but he didn't believe her. He was drunk and bottles were all over the floor. He blubbered and spat and pointed his finger. It made Mary scared, so she left. She didn't have money for a hotel, so having nowhere else to go, she called the rich man. He invited her to stay the night.

Mary slept in one of the guest rooms, to be proper. But she wondered how warm his bed was.

She went back home the following morning. Her husband still snored on the couch from all the drinking. Mary cleaned up the bottles and vacuumed the floors and didn't care how much noise she made. None of it woke him.

And as Mary looked at his sorry state, she wondered how she got here. He was one of the first men she met when she came to the country. He was kind and sweet, if not a little distracted. At the time, she wondered if it was a cultural thing. It took Mary too long to see that it wasn't—not until some time after they were married. He changed almost immediately after their honeymoon. The effort slowed and stopped until she was more like a mother than a wife. And in this moment, Mary realized she had let it carry on for years.

Conversely, she looked at the rich man and his wife. He was always taking her to things and giving her gifts, even after they had been married for decades. Their house was huge and he had a job where he was powerful and envied. How could that not be enough for her? It would be more than enough for Mary. The rich man would be so much better than the slobbering excuse slumped along the couch.

The thought angered Mary, so she left the house before the cleaning was done. She was tired of looking after her useless husband. She was tired caring for him like a child. She was tired of begging him to pick himself up when all he wanted to do was lay around.

Not like the rich man. He was a real man—respectable, successful, and smart.

So she went back to the rich man's house. And when he

opened the door, Mary kissed him.

He didn't expect it. He jumped in surprise, then sank into it. That showed Mary he had felt the same all these months—a passion bubbling below the surface, a pressure valve ready to burst. This was the eruption. He took Mary to the master bedroom and made love to her. Mary graced the bed that the rich man's wife had graced hundreds of nights before.

The rich man's divorce papers came in the mail several days later. He paced up and down the living room, wringing the papers in his hands, muttering to himself. Mary asked him what they said. He said his wife was trying to take him for everything. The house, the cars, the business, everything. She was accusing him of heinous things, things that weren't true, things that couldn't be true. Mary didn't ask him what. It didn't matter what he said—Mary believed him.

From that point, Mary spent as little time at home as possible. Her husband's accusation had become true—she was having an affair with the rich man. But she couldn't admit that to him, not now. So Mary let him go on believing and she went on denying. And as the days wore on, he became colder. But Mary didn't care. Silently, she was making her escape to be with the rich man.

Her escape became suddenly clear weeks later when the rich man presented an idea. He told Mary the divorce wouldn't go well. His wife was amassing a trove of lies that would surely rob him of everything. He had to act fast if he wanted to save himself, but he wanted Mary to come with him. He said he knew of a faraway place where they could build a new life together. A place where his wealth would let them live like royalty.

The thought excited and scared Mary. Leaving this country and starting somewhere fresh after she had fought so hard to get here sounded like a nightmare. But this time was different, because she wouldn't be alone. She'd have the rich man to guide and protect her. And he was just as determined and resourceful as she was.

Mary didn't have to think about it long. She said yes. She asked him when they would leave. He said the next day.

When Mary went home that night, her husband had suddenly changed. Gone was the obstinate, stubborn, lazy man that she knew. He had cleaned himself up. Bought her flowers. He said not having Mary around the house to look after him made him realize how much he needed her. And he realized how helpful he *hadn't* been for years. He promised to become better. He promised to change and find a job and be the support Mary always needed. He vowed things would be different.

Mary stood there, awestruck. She thought about telling him everything. She almost confessed to the affair with the rich man and her plans to leave with him the following morning. But she didn't. She went to bed with him that night and let him believe that she would still be there in the morning.

But Mary packed her suitcase and slipped away before the sun even broke the sky. She didn't leave a note. She simply disappeared. A spike of guilt buried in her chest, but she didn't know what else to do.

Mary and the rich man were airborne in his private jet by that afternoon. She had never been in a private jet before. The leather seats, the on-board meals… It was so decadent. She had almost grown used to fine things in the time she had spent with him, but this felt like another level of luxury.

Hours went by. Mary expected to land on an exotic island or somewhere in Europe, but she was mistaken.

They descended over a jungle—hills of thick, tropical foliage as far as she could see. They landed on a narrow strip of dirt carved out of the forest. When the plane hatch opened up, they were blasted with hot, humid air. Mary fanned her face and watched as some locals took their bags and escorted them to a nearby car. Their button-up shirts were coated with sweat and their faces glistened.

A feeling of unease clung to Mary, but her confidence in the rich man didn't waver. This was the start of a new life with a true partner by her side. The locals loaded Mary, the rich man, and their things into a van. But when the rich man counted the bags they put in the back, he burst into hysterics.

The rich man had counted five bags. There were supposed to be six. The crew said they only received five. The rich man said that couldn't be true, that they left home with six. The crew said they would check the plane later and send the remaining bag if it was there, but that the van was scheduled for another visitor soon and they had to take their ride. That was unacceptable to the rich man. He was furious, screaming and demanding to check the plane himself, but the crew members refused.

Mary sat quietly in the van, listening to the rich man's muffled screams. She had never seen him like this before—ruddy-faced, trembling, threatening. She didn't like it. He had always been so gentle and sweet. This was a side of him she didn't know existed. She dreaded the thought of being on the receiving end.

In a huff, the rich man joined Mary in the van and slammed the door. He still breathed like a gorilla, and he didn't look at his precious mistress. She put her hand on his knee, but he swatted it away. Mary put her hands on her lap and tried not to cry.

A few minutes later, when he was calmer, he told her in less than a whisper that all of their money was in that missing bag. That made Mary's blood turn cold.

They ventured into the jungle for over an hour. Then they arrived at a house. It was lovely from the outside, with a tall white fence that circled the property. Inside had a large front lawn with statues and overgrown grass. It clearly hadn't been cared for in a good while, but it wouldn't take too much to clean up, especially with the rich man's help.

The crew unloaded the belongings quickly. The rich man tried to get answers from them on when the missing baggage would arrive, and the crew gave him hurried and dismissive answers. Before Mary and the rich man knew it, the locals were speeding back down the road, leaving them with their five remaining bags.

Neither the rich man nor Mary said it, but they were certain they had just been robbed.

Silently, they crept into their new home. It was filled with beautiful furniture, but everything was dusty like it hadn't been touched in years. Mary said it would need cleaning. Bitterly, the rich man told Mary they had nothing to clean with. She told him we would figure it out together. He started yelling again, but this time, at her. He said there would be nothing to figure out. He had planned a one-way flight to this emergency home he had bought years ago, but now no one knew where they were, and they were completely out of money. He said they were going to die. He said it was hopeless. Then he stomped away.

Mary stood frozen in shock. It was one thing for him to yell at the crew for misplacing a suitcase full of money, but it was another thing for him to yell at *her*, his new love, the woman he escaped everything to be with. She was worried this was the man she now lived with.

She was right.

That was three years ago.

It became clearly visible to see why his wife was so bitter

and cold before the divorce. The rich man always had a mask on. Behind closed doors, under stress, when no one was watching, he became someone else. His kindness and humor evaporated. Instead, the man Mary thought she loved was a fragile lid atop a simmering pot of anger.

Now, most of the house's fine furniture is gone. They were lucky to find a village a half-day walk from the house soon after they arrived. They were able to barter the furniture as scrap wood. That earned them some food for a while. But you can only barter for so long with limited possessions. Mary finally traded some scrap wood for seeds and planted their own garden. She had to dig up the front yard to do it, planting staples like corn so they wouldn't starve.

The rich man doesn't do anything. He mostly wanders around the house or the forest, mumbling angrily, nursing cheap bottles of beer Mary can barely afford. He curses that flight crew that robbed him of his riches. He curses his ex-wife for starting this mess. He curses Mary, which is odd, considering he would die without her. Mary thought he was a man of tenacity and vision, and she was right. But not in the ways that matter now. Spreadsheets and portfolios do nothing in a jungle.

Mary often thinks of her husband back home—that promise he made the night before she fled. She wonders if he was sincere about changing or if he was desperate to win back her affection. Maybe he truly did turn himself around. Perhaps he's found a new wife and they have a child. Mary wonders if he thinks of her. She hopes he's happy. But she's given up on knowing.

PICTURES FOR TREES

As a legendary photojournalist, Sebastião Salgado visited countless countries documenting human suffering with dramatic black-and-white photography.

He's also turned thousands of barren acres into a lush, vibrant forest.

I first saw his work through an internet meme and I didn't know if it was real or not. You see so many things trickle down the endless Facebook doomscroll, it can be hard to tell what actually happened and what's fabricated by well-intentioned Sunday School teachers. But after some Google searches, I found out it was true.

Sebastião Salgado and his wife Lélia restored a forest.

The poetry of this situation is sweet to me, especially after reading about the process. The land was originally gifted to Sebastião by his father. Sebastião was underwhelmed by it, to say the least. At the time, the land was in terrible shape. Due to deforestation, it had become a long, barren stretch of scarred earth, devoid of life. It would be a massive undertaking to bring it back. But Sebastião and Lélia resolved to do it anyway.

They worked with some local organizations to secure plant funding. Sebastião even auctioned an exclusive titanium Leica M7 camera to help finance their efforts. That camera had probably seen the world and taken award-winning photos. It sold for over $100,000, all going toward the forest restoration initiative. About the funds it generated, Sebastião said, "One small camera, and we planted 30,000 trees."

After a decade of work, the barren land became a forest again. Where there was death and emptiness, there is now life. A new ecosystem for plants, animals, and insects. All through the tenacity of a photographer and his family.

Their efforts teach us that with time and effort, we can sow life over the scars of the past.

POEMS

Together and Apart

We are aspens.

Aspens are beautiful and singular, but not truly.

Their roots are woven together under the surface.

We may grow separately, but not truly.

We may spread apart, but not truly.

We'll always share the same roots.

Father's Day

Today, I found the final
birthday card and
Christmas card
you wrote me.

They were sleeping
in a box tucked in
a corner of
my closet.

It's now
the last thing I own
with your handwriting
on it.

How strange that
I would find it on a day
when I should be
celebrating you instead.

Life's Canvas

If there is no grand design,
all meaning is self-prescribed.

Does that make life pointless?

Not at all.

God, the Universe, or Fate,
has gifted us a blank slate.
A fresh canvas.
A space for something new.

In your hands is every color,
dripping from your fingertips,
waiting for your mind
to spread its wings.

So paint, then.
Be messy and loud.
Be bold and brash and bright
and big and dumb and free!

Your life is a work of art
and it's beautiful to me.

Indecision

She loves me,
she loves me not.

She's got herself
tied up in knots.

A friend or lover,
which do you want?

Don't pull me close,
then push me off.

Yellow Skin

You're not as strong
as you once were.

Gone is the frame
of a linebacker,
tall, strong, with
broad shoulders
and thick hands.

Now you're a flower
wilting away
in winter.

Your yellow skin sags
and your voice is hoarse.

You know the weather
is getting colder,
and you'll pass along
with the falling leaves.

I'll miss you when spring comes.

2:00 AM

My mind said "no" tonight.
The dreadful dark is a time to think,
not rest.

A time to
question my relationships or
recall humiliation or
let angry thoughts stew or
tumble through my feed or
read another chapter or
add items to the list.

Anything but sleep.

Big Love Daughter

I hate myself for wanting you.

You warned me you would bite,
I tried to hold you anyway.

You said your heart was closed,
I tried to win it anyway.

You made of me a joke,
I dealt you kindly anyway.

You made me feel minute,
I praised and soothed you anyway.

You turned your back on me,
I tried to reach you anyway.

I should have listened.

Edith

Two hours and a few buttons
taught me that death and madness
are always a few steps away and that
families are a beautiful curse.

For Joe

How?
How?
Whether it's

floating castles or
bath houses or
flying pigs or
forest spirits

your songs stir magic
that glides on air
and lifts my soul.

The Irony of Unfathomable Power

When you have everything,
nothing is special.

The only thing in abundance
is hunger.

The Last Hug

You stood to hug me before you died.

You forced yourself to stand
just so you could
wrap your arms around me.

You could barely speak.
You could barely move.

But you stood up to hug me.

You might as well have climbed a mountain.

Warmth in Late October

It gets dark at 6 o'clock.
I'm bundled in my hoodie and jeans
with a belly full of hot cider
and shoes crunching on the dirt.

But your laughs are infectious
and your little touches are sweet,
effortlessly thoughtful and
without guile.

For years, I thought this kind of love
was something out of reach.
Not physical affection,
but to be truly seen.

You let me know without speaking
that I am a part of you,
and that I am accepted
as I am, faults and all.

And that keeps me warmer
than the cider.

Sunday Scaries

It's been so long but I've got Sunday Scaries again and now it's 5:37pm and I'm wondering how I should spend the rest of my evening because I should probably relax but I also want to get things done and it's hard to find this happy medium because I've already read a book today so that's a nice balance but I should probably also meal prep and write in my journal and call my parents but maybe I'll watch a movie because that's relaxing but then what do I choose because I could watch something I've seen or watch something new but what if I watch something new and I don't like it then that will be a waste of time and oh my gosh I still have to go to work tomorrow and I need to get groceries after work tomorrow but I should also write in this book after work tomorrow but there's still aaahhhh work tomorrow why do I have to work why can't I just get paid for being a relatively pleasant person instead of having to go to work tomorrow and I still haven't picked a movie to watch tonight before I have to go to work tomorrow I have to go to work tomorrow I have to go to work tomorrow

Foggy Day

The cloud comes down
to make a haze
that dampens my eyes
that brushes my face

The distance is gone,
now there is only *here*.

Is that a problem?
Perhaps not.

A little voice tells me
there is wisdom in this.

Overthinking

These thoughts are shackles and wings
that help me soar
and make me crash.

When The Bell Tolls

There's a clock in the living room
that chimes every hour.

Bong! Bong! Bong!

A small hammer rings out a
shimmering note.

The chimes, loud and bright,
always fade.

Although not completely.

Your life will be the same.

You may shed this mortal vessel,
but our memories will
still ring on.

So you'll never really die.
Not truly.

Paradox

Leave me alone—
but don't leave me lonely.

Time

Time is cruel and fickle
because we built it ourselves
but it's the ice on which
everything slides.

Time keeps marching but it's
just a turning rock
as it glides through
endless black.

Time shouldn't dictate
how people come and go
and I remain
the same.

Time shouldn't ravage
things that are lovely
with reckless
rust and decay.

But the earth keeps turning

and time keeps lurching

and I remain the same.

Seasons

Poems of autumn are
warm and bright and
hold you close.

Poems of winter are
biting cold and
dreadful still.

Poems of spring are
pale and soft and
give new life.

Poems of summer are
high and loud and
gone too soon.

Unpacking

It doesn't matter
that your dad died,

that you'll never feel his hugs
or hear his voice again,

when you get home,
you still have to unpack.

3:00 AM

I thought I was done loving you
until I saw you in
another's arms.

Now these sheets are
cold and empty
and sleep has
fled my eyes.

You bring me in and push me back,
ask to stay, sit and wait,
and hang upon your time.

I know this fire is dead,
but I can't forget the coals.

Awake Now

I arrived at
last at what
I hold to be
the truth.

I was only
in love with
the idea
of you.

The Earth Says No

There's a crack
in the asphalt under
a part someone
tarred over.

A crevice opened up
like an old wound
beneath it,
fighting back.

Someone tried to apply
that black,
rubbery bandage,
but the earth said no.

The earth always says no.

A Father's Love

A father's love is a beautiful sword
that shimmers and gleams
and tears asunder.

The hugs and kisses and I-love-yous
are sweet and real because
they're truly sincere.

But they always came after
the terrible silence
and sharp words.

Never enough,
never enough,
never enough,
I always believed

because of a father's love.

Things That Feel The Same

November
Thursday
8:00 PM
Gray clouds
Page 9 of 10

The held breath
before the end.

In Between

The in between place
is the worst to be.

The past is now the past
and falling out of reach.

But the future waits on the
cusp of something that
you cannot see.

All that's left to do is
close your eyes, hold your breath,
and wait.

The worst place to be
is the in between.

Regrets

I asked him if he had any
as he wasted away.

He mentioned the time he
turned his face from God.

That was the only regret.

There was no mention of
the fear he built in us
from the times he worked
late nights or failed
to squelch his temper.

There was no mention
of the times he made us cry.

Those never crossed his mind.

Nowhere To Go

If grief is just love with nowhere to go,

is grief the only thing I've ever known?

Autumn

It's the time when the earth sighs
and the sun is calm and cool

The time of creaking rocking chairs
and crispy, crunchy leaves

The summer's gnash has gone to bed
And winter still is snoring

So I smile and dress warm for a
lovely autumn's morning

Dead Dad Jokes

It's kind of fun
to watch you squirm.

A father's grave
is a lemon,

but you can still make
tasty lemonade.

Just add lots of
sugar.

A Poem From My Morning Walk

I thought of a poem today on my morning walk.
I don't know what it is yet,
but the air was sweet and sun was warm
and to me, it felt worthy
of a line or two.

The world is quietly beautiful
and for that, I am thankful.

Where Should I Put This Woodpecker?

Where should I put this woodpecker?
It's gnawing and scratching so fierce.
And just when I think that it's finally died,
it's freshly assaulting my ears.

It seemingly came out of nowhere.
I never once heard it before.
But now it's so near and it won't disappear
with its racket I strongly abhor.

It grants me some peace for a moment.
The forest and wind breathe a sigh.
But then comes that bird so abundantly heard
And makes my emotions run high.

Maybe I need to be patient
And learn to find peace in the noise.
The woodpecker drills, but the echoes grow still
And in that, I can somehow rejoice.

Birthday

I found those cards again
while I was unpacking.

Yesterday I didn't get to hear you
harmonize "Happy Birthday"
while you sang with Mom.

I didn't get a birthday card
with one of your silly
drawings in it.

I decided to let myself be sad
and the tears came quickly.

I yearned to feel your arms around me,
feeling safe in your embrace.

Happy birthday to me.

Change

There are trees out my window now,
a tall, cottonwood fence.

It's early November and their leaves
shiver with the breeze.

Reds, yellows, and browns
trickle to the ground
as winter approaches.

Strange how trees, without thoughts or worries,
still prepare for what's to come.

The Student's Proverb

Dead masters
can't deny
their wisdom.

Learn from those
who laid the
ground for you.

That Old Record

I used to love that record.

I called it raw and real.

My love for it is gone.

Now it's harsh and loud.

Too Heavy

I don't feel like writing anything.
The world is too heavy.

The nation is crumbling
and the winter is dreadful
and this house is so empty
and there's too much to do.

I want to sleep, but
my worries plague my eyes.

I don't feel like writing anything.

Thanksgiving

It wasn't as bad as we thought.

Mom had the kitchen to herself
because you weren't there to help her.

I tried to lend a hand, but
she was only doing the
turkey and the stuffing,
so she had it covered.

Everyone else brought a little something.
We lightened the load together.

And in the end, there was plenty of love in the room.

Watermelon

It's not sane
to burn a building
when a few tenants
have wronged you.

Flames grow, mothers flee,
children starve, and the world watches.

We cry and shout but
leaders shrug and
count their stocks
and vomit lies.

Retelling the tragedy
that lives mean nothing
when they're far enough away.

Those Who Defy The Silence

As I crested the hill
I saw scores of people
gathered en mass
singing for freedom

My heart pricked and
the tears swelled
because for once
my heart burned bright

We would not shrink,
we would not fold,
or fade into
a helpless night

Our voice as one
will keep us free.
Our voice as one
will keep us free.

For the Homies

Most of you
don't have a way with words,
but I sure do.

Here's some things
that you can say to earn
a smooch or two.

The stars may turn cold
and the sun may cease its light,
but my love for you
will live on.

God could have put me anywhere at any time,
but He put me here with you,
my favorite place of all.

DAMN SHAWTY WHAT THAT THING DO?

Your arms are a cleansing bath
that awakens my soul
and brings me to light.

I could live a thousand years
and my ardent admiration for you
would never dim or fade.

BRING THAT THING OVER HERE GUURRLL

Christmas

We made it easy on ourselves again.

We didn't open presents until 1pm
so we could sleep in
and take it slow.

We kept it light. Money was tight for everyone.

Kristin made the lemon poppy seed bread
you would always make.
It smelled just like the original.

We had a light lunch of Hawaiian roll sandwiches
with potato chips and sides of fruit and veggies.

It was enough. We still missed you.

Content

My appetite for love was slaked
when I learned that I am
truly, undeniably, irrefutably
enough.

SHOPPING LISTS

Shopping List #1

Groceries
- Salisbury steak TV dinners
- Cereal
- Milk
- Copy of *Mad Scientist Monthly*

Doomsday Device
- Uranium (maybe they keep it in the back?)
- Three tons of steel (may have to order in)
- Nail gun
- Arc welder
- Swivel chair

Shopping List #2

Groceries
- Cereal
- Milk
- Frozen pizzas

Doomsday Device
- Uranium (follow up with store clerk)
- Cushion for swivel chair
- Computer monitor
- 50-caliber gatling gun with self-cooling mechanism
- Cup holder (might be in auto section)

Shopping List #3

Groceries
- Cereal
- Milk
- Frozen chicken pot pies
Doomsday Device
- Uranium (has it arrived yet??)
- New swivel chair (back pain from last one)
- Tanks for Uranium
- Toaster oven (can retrofit into heat ray)
- Pressure washer (for toxic waste spray)
- Ergonomic keyboard

Shopping List #4

Groceries
- Cereal
- Milk
- TV Dinners
- Cologne
- Flowers and chocolates (for Esther, the lady I met at the store)

Doomsday Device
- Uranium (give a stern talking to the manager)
- New pressure washer (last one melted)
- 50-gallon plastic tubs
- Really big bluetooth speaker (for playing threatening music)
- Standing desk

Shopping List #5

Groceries
- Milk
- Cereal
- 1 lb of ground beef
- Wild rice
- Chicken broth
- Copy of *Mad Scientist Monthly*
- *Gilmore Girls* on DVD (Esther wants to watch for date night)

Doomsday Device
- Uranium (WHERE IS IT)
- Nail gun (last one failed)
- Old-timey bombs (do they still make these?)
- Gasoline
- Flame thrower

Shopping List #6

Groceries
- Salsa
- Chicken breasts
- Black beans
- Tortillas
- Painting supplies (for *Gilmore Girls* nights)

Doomsday Device
- Uranium (this is getting ridiculous)
- More gasoline
- Ammo for 50 caliber weapon (how could I forget??)
- Copper wire
- Spinney spikey things

Shopping List #7

Groceries
- TV dinners
- Vapor rub
- Chicken soup
- Get Well Soon card for Esther
Doomsday Device
- Uranium (maybe the clerk lied to me)
- Mouse pad
- Anti-matter collector
- Really really really big red button

Shopping List #8

Groceries
- Frozen tater tots
- 1 lb of ground beef
- Grated cheddar cheese
- Cream of mushroom soup
- Peachy ring candies (Esther loves these <3)
Doomsday Device
- Uranium (find from different seller)
- Coolant
- Circuit board
- Housing for circuit board

Shopping List #9

Groceries
- Pizza dough
- Peppers
- Olives
- Low sodium pizza sauce
- Mozzarella cheese
- Shelf for all the action figures Esther gave me
- Copy of *Mad Scientist Monthly*
Doomsday Device
- Uranium
- Housing for electrical unit
- Hazmat suit

Shopping List #10

Groceries
- Rice
- Chicken
- Frozen broccoli
- Protein powder
- Tickets to that musical Esther loves (surprise!!)
- Patches for the cool jacket Esther got me
Doomsday Device
- Uranium
- Garden hose

Shopping List #11

Groceries
- Swim trunks for Esther's vacation
- Sun screen
- Flip flops
- Beach towel
- Carry-size water cooler
- Esther's healthy sodas

Doomsday Device
- Uranium (it's finally in!!)

Shopping List #12

Groceries
- Crockpot (no more borrowing Esther's)
- Pot roast
- Beef broth
- Potatoes
- Carrots
- Flowers for Esther

Shopping List #13

Groceries
- Potatoes
- Vegetable oil
- Eggs
- Garlic
- 1 lb ground beef
- Sour cream
- 2 copies of *The Fae's Desire* (Esther wants to read it together)

Shopping List #14

Groceries
- Apples
- Bananas
- Baby spinach
- Mixed berries
- Stretchy workout bands (for Esther and I)

To-Do List

- Return Uranium (no longer needed)
- Donate all doomsday device things to community colleges (scatter them so I don't look suspicious)
- Cancel subscription to *Mad Scientist Monthly*
- Pick up engagement ring for Esther

THANK YOU FOR READING!!

Please leave a review of this book wherever you leave reviews! Indie authors live and die by the reviews—it helps us build credibility and reach more readers. So if you loved *Where Should I Put This Woodpecker?*, please tell someone! Thank you!!

ACKNOWLEDGMENTS

It takes a small army to make a great book. I'm nothing without the following people.

First, thank you to all my beta readers: Tim Costello, Audrie Hopper, Rebecca Keele, Angela Rigby, and James Hagan Jr. Their feedback helped me tighten up these stories, poems, and shopping lists.

Second, thank you to Leah Taylor, my wonderful editor! She's so quick and thorough and leaves delightful little notes to let you know what works and what doesn't. She rules.

Third, thank you to Ryan Bouche, Claire Sorensen, Zaylie Reynolds, and Caleb Baldwin for their feedback on the book cover. I'm not a designer, but I wanted to push myself creatively and take a stab at it with this book. I'm satisfied with how it turned out. As experienced designers, their professional feedback got me in the right direction.

I also want to thank my dad for kicking the bucket. If he didn't croak, this book wouldn't have been the same. Thanks, dad. (Chill out, he would have thought this part was funny.)

Lastly, I want to thank you, dear reader. Thanks for picking this up! Thanks for reading my silly, sad little stories and poems! I hope they made you feel something, and I hope you loved them so much you go buy every book I've ever written. I do this all for you. Consider yourself high-fived.

ABOUT THE AUTHOR

Photo by Adam Anderson

Aaron N. Hall is the author of *The Legend of Uh*, The Wevlian Chronicles, the Hammerfist Series, and several collections of stories and poems. When he's not writing (which isn't often), he's doing nonprofit work, lifting heavy things, reading a book, or sipping a cup of tea. He lives in Utah.

Join the Insiders Guild on aaronnhall.com for special notifications on Aaron's work.

OTHER BOOKS BY AARON N. HALL

The Legend of Uh

THE WEVLIAN CHRONICLES
Foreordained
Purged
Awakened

THE HAMMERFIST SERIES
My Name is Hammerfist
My Name is Hammerfist Vol. 2

OTHER COLLECTIONS
*I'm Sorry, Here's a Plasma Rifle: A Collection of Stories,
Poems, and Pastry Recipes*
*Love Letters to a House on Fire: Stories, Poems, and
Ransom Notes*